# THE
# SIGN
## OF THE
# ARROW

*The Sign of the Arrow is the third book in Stephen Brooke's fantasy epic,
Donzalo's Destiny, following the events
in The Song of the Sword and The Shadow of Asak.*

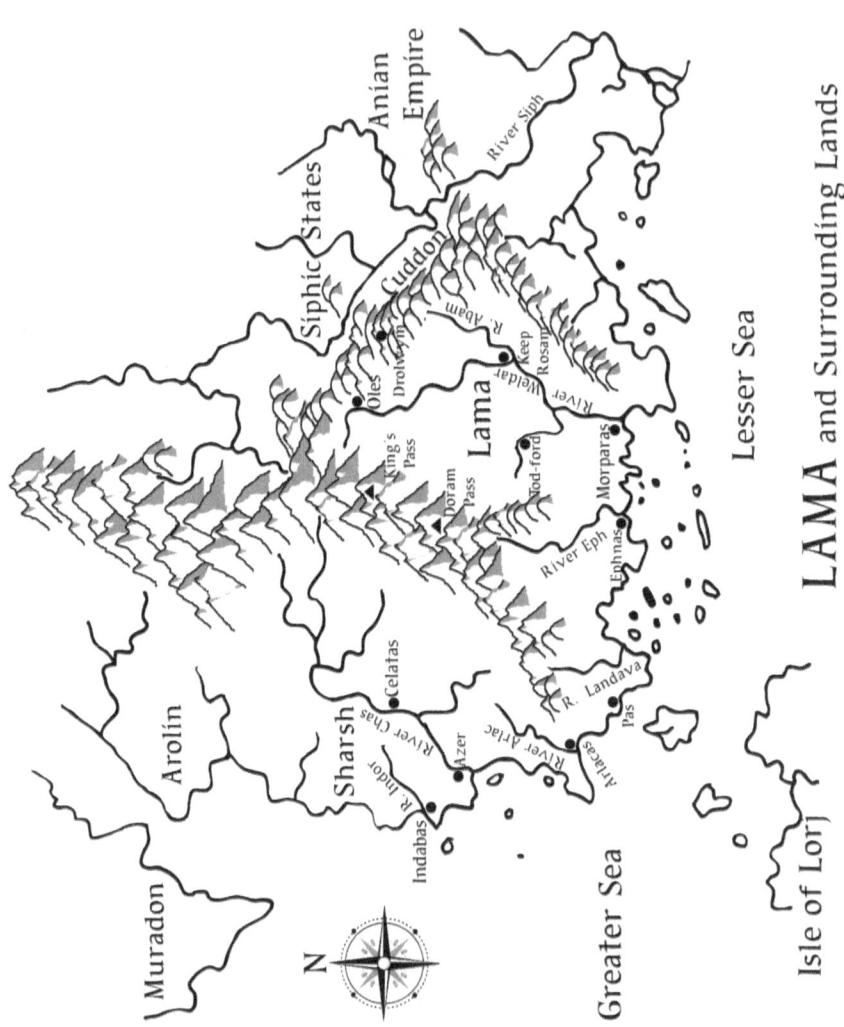

# THE SIGN OF THE ARROW

## STEPHEN BROOKE

Arachis Press 2014

*To the journeys that come!*

The Sign of the Arrow
©2014 Stephen Brooke

ISBN 978-1-937745-15-8

Arachis Press
4803 Peanut Road
Graceville, FL 32440
http://arachispress.com

# OF DAUGHTERS: THE SIXTH TALE

## 1

A town of tents had sprung up beside the Weldar, some garishly colored and some plain, striped tents and tents of solid hue and some seemingly sewn together of whatever material came to hand. The Spring Fair was in as full a bloom as the flowers that carpeted the surrounding hills, and would continue yet a fortnight, to conclude at the May Festival.

"This is nothing compared to the Summer Fair," Donzalo told his companions. "There will be twice this many, aye, and more than that."

"I have done business at Borrago's Summer Fair these past two years. There is none larger, at least that I know of," said Galaro.

His brother gazed out over the field in wonder. "In the Siphic states, they think Lama is a land of bumpkins, and backward in all things. They are, it seems, much misinformed. As," he continued, shaking his head, "am I."

"We shall do our best to remedy that, Sir Habidros," stated Corgos, titular Captain of this small troop, though all looked to young Donzalo as their true leader. "We had best get on to the keep. The sooner we can report to the count that Donzalo is safely home, the better."

"And the sooner to see your new wife again," jested one of the men at arms he had brought with him from Castle Rosam, to chuckles all around. Along the road south, Sir Corgos had made no attempt to hide his eagerness to again be with his bride.

Donzalo looked toward his home, perched on the heights above the town, the home he had left but two seasons ago. Those seasons seemed now like years. "Then let us finish this journey," he spoke, spurring his horse forward.

~ ~ ~

"So." Oder, Anian spy-master, pondered the story Guesare had told him, then raised his sky-blue eyes to regard the man who had been protege, friend, lover. "You are correct that it makes no difference, for now. Still, it would have been a fact worth knowing."

The minstrel shrugged. "And now you know it. When the child is older I am sure you will have all sorts of plots in place."

Oder shook his head. "Donzalo the father of his brother's heir — it is amusing, truly."

"It didn't amuse young Donzalo very much to be the target of assassins. Now you have the last piece of that particular puzzle."

The Anian paused, momentarily baffled by the reference. Jigsaw puzzles had not been part of life on the steppes where he had grown up nor of his experiences as a spy since.

But, being a spy, he was quick to catch the intended meaning behind words. "Yes. This needs be a secret known to a very few. Perhaps you did well to guard it.

"Now, all this you have learned of Radal's daughter — some I knew, some I did not. I was aware that Fachalana had become her father's apprentice, thanks to my spy in Celatas." He took a piece of paper into his hand. "I have her latest report here."

Guesare waited, expecting him to hand it over, but Oder chose not to and replaced it on the tavern table before him.

"Her?" asked the Cuddonian minstrel.

"Yes. I have my own little secrets, Guesare, and I think I will let you in on this one. Even if," he chided, "you were not as forthcoming as I might have wished about Donzalo."

Guesare chose to ignore his friend's accusation, knowing it not serious. He waited for Oder to continue.

"You have met my agent. You knew her as Posena." Oder smiled at the minstrel's reaction.

"She was your creature? I was much puzzled by her," he said, narrowing his eyes, "and the reasons for her presence at Castle Rosam."

6

"Those reasons were not mine, though I willingly approved her plan. She was there to further the plots of her friend and patroness, the Lady Fachalana. In Celatas, my young spy is known as the actress Maresta."

"This grows tangled," observed Guesare. "Who is the girl, truly?"

"Ah, I think Donzalo glimpsed something of her true identity. He is an observant one." Oder beckoned to the barmaid, gossiping at the door with a passer-by. "Two more tankards of that fine dark beer, girl."

The Anian watched with obvious appreciation as she went to fetch their brew. Guesare could not help but feel a twinge of jealousy.

It was a small tavern in a small town along the Siphic Road, and a favored haunt of the spy-master. Ostensibly, these rugged hills — the northern end of the Cuddon — that divided the valleys of the Weldar and Siph were a part of the Anian Empire. In practice, the Ani left the people here to rule themselves and were content to simply keep the road open.

Oder drank deeply. "There won't be much more of this brew until next spring. It's the main reason I chose this town for our rendezvous."

Guesare knew they were accustomed to seeing Anians here, making it useful as a meeting place, as well as being well-located for sending out spies into Lama and beyond. He remained silent — the man across the table from him enjoyed his little games of manipulation but the minstrel could choose not to play.

"The girl is, of course, of my people," spoke Oder. "Her name is Ansa." He paused to take another quaff from his tankard, then added in a low, matter-of-fact tone, "She is my sister.

"Donzalo may have recognized the kinship between us when we were traveling together. He suspected something — I could see it in his eyes."

The normally loquacious minstrel could think of nothing to say.

Oder knew well the odd mix of the complex and the simple that made up his friend. A momentary wistfulness filled him as he leaned back and regarded the minstrel, still a young man but no longer the boy he had taken under his wing. Then, such thoughts were quickly swept away in favor of the business at hand. "Your paths may well cross again. Possibly soon. You will head to County Rosam, now?"

Guesare nodded. "I should be there for Summer Feast." He gulped down the dark brew in his flagon. "Could we have some wine, now?"

~ ~ ~

"Whom do you serve, Captain Nordoc? Hmmm." Lady Fachalana looked up from the page she held. "Whom do *you* serve, Captain Nordoc?"

Ansa nodded her approval. "Yes, yes. An accusation, almost."

"Not that it matters," replied the tall young noblewoman. "I do not intend to play the role."

"Better you than I. You cut a far more heroic figure."

Fachalana smiled at her petite companion. "But you are the better actress, Maresta," she asserted, knowing the woman still by that name. Throwing the sheaf of papers onto the table, she took a seat. "The play is not finished enough to mount, anyway. We will not attempt it this season."

"Then we'd best choose another to finish out our spring. And try to get Lector Nafal to complete this one to our satisfaction."

Fachalana shifted her weight on the hard wooden chair. I should bring some cushions, she told herself. She had told herself this before yet never remembered to do it. "Jobareth is halfway to Lama by now. We need to sit down with him and work it out."

"Then, my lady," replied her friend, with a ghost of a smile, "all the more reason for us to go visit him there."

"Shall we take our company on the road, as do so many others in the summer?" Fachalana had actually been giving the idea some idle thought. All who could deserted Celatas during the hottest months and most theaters would close until autumn. It was a good time to tour.

"All the way to County Rosam?" asked Ansa. "I must warn you

that Lama is dreadfully hot in the summer. It is not at all like touring in the uplands here." Mountain villages — especially those that lay near the summer homes of the aristocracy — were the preferred venue of most roving companies.

"Well, then just the two of us," decided Fachalana, "and whatever retinue on which my father insists."

"If he permits it, at all."

"He will, I think," said the noblewoman. Both suspected that Lord Radal had hidden reasons for allowing his daughter to visit Lama. Neither chose to voice her suspicion.

"What of 'The Purloined Pigeon' to close out the season?" said Fachalana, of a sudden.

"A comedy, my lady?"

"Yes, and you in the lead." She became emphatic — passions easily and quickly took hold of Fachalana. "It is more than time that you played such a role. We can not have you forever cast as the villain! But," she added, her smile signaling another change in mood, "you may need to dye that blond hair."

Ansa nodded. It would be nice to be the heroine, she told herself, if only in make-believe.

~ ~ ~

"Pol! What do you here?"

"Sir Blen sent me, Lector, to await you here at Mountain Keep and to accompany you on the way back." The young soldier laughed. "And to get me where I would not be nosing about, eh?"

A not too subtle message that he knew Pol was Jobareth's man, the diplomat told himself. They stood in one of the many passages that honeycombed the fortress, some built upon the mountain rock and some carved into it.

"You should address me now as Legate," he said to the boy. "Yes, I've been promoted. This is my secretary, Benawis. Him you call Lector."

He turned to his aide. "Pol, I suppose, could be considered my sergeant, had I any other soldiers in my troop." These two are nearly of an age, thought Jobareth. Benawis may have lived a year or two more but has had little experience of the world. I should treat them as equals and hope they do the same. "In fact, I officially confer that rank on you right now, Sergeant Pol.

"You should move to our quarters. We are searching for them now."

"I know where they are, sir. I moved into them when I arrived two days ago." Pol turned to lead the way up the corridor. "Is the new ambassador with you?"

Benawis looked both scandalized and amused by the soldier's informal manner. "He's been among Lamans too long," Jobareth whispered. "You'll have to become accustomed to it there. He's a good lad," he continued, "and you'll do well to make him a friend."

"Yes, Legate. I met him when you both arrived here from Lama."

"Oh." This Jobareth had not known. Some things must be beyond ones control and the first encounter of these two had been one of them. "Yes, Sergeant," he said more loudly, "the Lord Doufan has accompanied us. He is paying his respects to the reeve of the keep."

## 2

"The Lady Vibola passed quietly in her sleep," Doctor Heragos told Donzalo. He pulled his long robes up as they began to ascend the stairway. "Your grandmother did live long enough to see the new baby."

"The child is not well, I have been told."

"No, Sir Donzalo, she is not." The pair spoke no further until they reached Lady Lomela's door. It stood ajar.

"I suggested that the air be allowed to pass through her chambers. 'Tis healthier," whispered Heragos, "and more so now that the days grow hot."

A round face appeared in the opening. "I thought I heard someone out here," said Mistress Traspa, in a subdued voice. "Welcome home, Master Donzalo."

She pulled the door open to them.

Unexpectedly, not only Lomela sat in the room, this room that was once so familiar to Donzalo, but his brother, Bolos, as well. The latter rose to greet him.

"I heard you were back. You've been with Father?"

"Just coming from him. How are you, Brother?" The two briefly and, perhaps a bit stiffly, clasped hands. They had never in all their lives embraced.

"Well enough, Donni, well enough." The words seemed unconvincing to Donzalo. He noted that his sibling had lost more weight and had the appearance of a man worn by worries.

The young knight bowed toward Lomela, who had come to her husband's side. "Greetings to you, my lady."

"And to you, Donzalo. *Sir* Donzalo," she corrected herself. "We must remember your brother is now a knight," she told Bolos.

A sour expression passed across the older man's face; as quickly, it was replaced by an impassive one. He only nodded.

No one cares that he is, as well, thought Donzalo. He has no tales of derring-do to follow him about.

Heragos broke in. "Might I look in on the child, my lady?"

"Of course, Doctor. As you suggested, we are being certain she has fresh air." She went to the girl's crib, beneath a window opening to the courtyard below. The doctor followed and laid his hand on the baby's head and then on her chest. He put his ear to a hearing-trumpet and listened to her breathing. He pulled at the tuft of beard on his chin and shook his head.

"She seems no better, gentlefolk. I am sorry."

Bolos sighed and put an arm around his wife. He feels this deeply, thought Donzalo, a bit surprised to recognize the ache in his brother's heart and an answering empathy in his own. He has cleaned up his life and this has been his reward.

The knight remembered his own loss then, the emptiness within him where once his Jola had been. Without thinking, Donzalo put his hand to the silver brooch at his shoulder. It seemed to reassure him.

He made his subdued goodbyes and found his way to his own long-unoccupied quarters.

~ ~ ~

"We will not again attempt an ambush."

"That seems wise," came Lareth's dry response, "considering your record." The king turned his head toward a young woman seated in the corner, quietly embroidering. "Will you leave us, my dear? But do be sure to return later."

She departed in a rustling of blue satin.

Radal looked askance at his monarch. "A new mistress?" he asked.

"Only a dalliance. The Lady Lis will remain at my side until the day one or the other of us is buried." Lareth gave a wry laugh. "We might as well be married, were it not politically unwise."

The king's councilor did not comment. He knew his liege had never let his love for his wives or, now, his mistress, get in the way of his love for all other women.

"So the boy will be home again," mused Lareth, King of Sharsh. "I would assume you have agents there."

"Yes, sire." Lord Radal did not mention that he had been unable to place anyone in Keep Rosam itself. Observers in the town — or embassy — would have to do. "Security has grown tight there and Borrago has most certainly grown cool towards us."

"That is not surprising. But we have done what was needed."

"We have tried to do what was needed, my king," replied the dark noble, "and failed. Again and again, we have failed." Lareth noted the barely suppressed bitterness in the man. This was not at all like his old friend.

"We can not have the Rosam allying themselves with Count Orgelo and this wedding is a threat to all our plans," Radal continued. His vehemence was now unconcealed.

The king was taken aback. "You would have us move against Borrago?" Surely, the man would not think to act so rashly.

"Remove the father and his whelp stands unprotected." The sorcerer's tone softened as he went on. "You said, my lord, that you would yourself lead an army into Lama were it necessary."

"And it is not yet necessary, my friend." Had this become personal for Radal? wondered the king. "Watch and wait. You leave in the morning?"

"Yes, sire. I can watch and wait, as you say, more effectively from Mountain Keep."

Lareth nodded his agreement. Then, turning their conversation to a lighter matter, he said, "I understand your daughter will be joining you there."

"Yes, my liege, as soon as she closes her theater for the summer. If all seems well, she will travel on to visit your own daughter. And," added the nobleman with an increasingly rare smile, "the man I hope to be her future husband."

"Well, join me in a goblet of wine, Radal, and before you must leave we shall drink to all good futures." The king himself poured out their libations and handed the cup to his friend and one-time protege.

If he will not act, I shall, the Lord Radal told himself later as he walked purposefully away from the king's chambers.

And in those chambers, the king wondered if his life-long friend and councilor should be removed from his duties.

~ ~ ~

Perdos rested in the shade of a sandstone outcropping, as his horse grazed one of the meadows scattered through this forest of oaks and of tall hickories, and thought on the reasons he hated the bard Guesare. He had much time to think of such things as he skulked in the wilds above Castle Rosam, near the borders of the Cuddon. If he remained here long enough, surely the man would return and he would have his chance at him.

Until then, he would live the life of a hunter, on the move and on the watch.

Guesare had slain his brother, Percos, of course. That was bad enough, though admittedly a fair fight. It was how he had instigated the whole affair, tricking the boy into dueling with him.

That had been politics, Perdos now realized. The brothers' dealings with Sharsh and Lord Radal had been at the bottom of it. If only they had kept away from intrigue and the promise of easy money, and had remained honest — well, mostly honest — soldiers.

That was another sore spot. Thanks to Guesare he had been banned from County Rosam and lost his comfortable post in Sir Bolos's retinue. Here he was, now, a homeless wanderer in the hills.

But most of all it was his own arm that reminded him of his hatred. He lay awake nights, feeling the pain in his shattered shoulder, knowing the only way to ever make it feel better would be to plunge a sword into the cocky Cuddonian.

Then, maybe, he could rest. I'll go back to that little inn, he told himself, when this is done. I'll settle down. I'll raise horses and take a wife and grow fat.

Perdos thought frequently of such things.

~ ~ ~

"Can you find me a cook, Marmoyo? Taking our meals at inns will no longer do when we move into the new embassy."

The Sharshites' agent pondered the request as though it were a question of great import. "Will you need more staff than just a cook, Sir Blen?" he inquired.

"I've already hired from the countryside locals. Every mason and carpenter who has worked on the place has relatives looking for a job. We need someone more sophisticated to prepare the ambassador's meals."

The Laman nodded knowingly. "You will be out of here soon, then?"

"Within the fortnight, Master Marmoyo, be the embassy finished or not. As promised." Blen rose from his chair, a signal for his visitor to do the same. "Have you made progress on my other request?" he asked.

"Indeed, sir, I have found several smaller houses that might do." He looked about the room. "The rent on this building is quite reasonable. You would not save much."

"It is too well known now as our residence. We desire a more private place where one of us can do business while in town, or stay over, if need be."

The two crossed the near-empty room to the doorway. "You can show me what you have found on the morrow. No, make that the day after. I must ride up to inspect the construction today and then on to Castle Rosam. Young Donzalo has returned and I should pay my respects."

"I bid you farewell then, sir," said the Laman, descending from the porch to the muddy streets of Ros-town.

Visiting the keep was not a task for which Blen cared. He would be happy to see Jobareth and the ambassador arrive so they could take over the work of diplomacy. For the last few months, all had fallen on the capable shoulders of the knight. Even those shoulders could grow tired.

~ ~ ~

Something was amiss here.

Indeed, Fachalana had felt something was amiss since she had risen that morning, knowing it was imperative that she visit her childhood friend, Prince Modareth and his new bride.

She had spent the previous evening trying to establish a link with her father, as he traveled toward the Mountain Keep. It had not gone well; Radal faded in and out of her trance-vision, their attempt at communication resulting only in disjointed and meaningless syllables.

It was she, though, who had been fading in and out. Fachalana knew this. She had not been able to hold to the link, to keep herself in that other place where they might meet. For that was how it worked, according to her father: their own physical being partially entered into other realms where they might come together.

All that talk of spirits and such was nonsense, he had told her. Wizardry meant learning to control ones passage into and through the myriad worlds other than our own, to be able to find what was needed in them — and to use it.

Fachalana had at last abandoned the attempt, knowing it was her own lack of discipline that caused her to drift away from her father's link. Her anger and frustration led to fitful, half-awake dreaming.

In the night, it seemed as if someone were speaking in another room. Not her father, a different voice, but with some of the same authority. A god? she wondered. She would like to meet a god someday.

Then she slept, but woke with the conviction that the prince was in danger.

She had been planning to say goodbye to Modi, anyway, before leaving Sharsh. Now Fachalana stood at the door of his dwelling, the small villa that he and Carrana had moved into following their wedding. It was really rather close to her father's home. She should have visited before.

Yes, something was amiss but this was not the foreboding she had felt earlier. Someone was clearing groaning on the other side of the door.

An unlocked door, the noblewoman found, when she placed her hand upon it. The red-lacquered slab swung open to reveal Modareth's single attendant and bodyguard spread prone on the floor, his blood flowing into the mortared joints between the tiles.

At that moment, Fachalana dearly wished she had brought her sword.

There was a dagger at the dying — probably dead, now — guard's waist. That would have to do. She slipped it from its sheath and hurried up the hallway.

## 3

Later, the Lady Fachalana realized that she had never hesitated. That fact quite astounded her when she thought upon it.

Up the passage she had gone, knife in hand, to face whatever danger threatened her friends. Yes, friends, for she now counted the Princess Carrana as such.

She heard a shriek, a quite blood-curdling shriek, and rushed toward the sound. Carrana? No, it had been the cook. The woman had apparently fainted and now lay upon the floor, pieces of a broken platter and an assortment of sweet cakes scattered about her.

Beyond her stood a man, a poniard in each hand, his back to Fachalana. And beyond him stood the royal couple. A late breakfast was spread on the table between them and the assassin.

Years of training — and much natural talent — had made Fachalana a skilled fencer. She could best most men with a dueling foil.

And that had not been enough for her so she had also studied the saber and the longsword and, yes, the dagger.

The man turned to face her with a sneer. His face seemed familiar but the noblewoman had no time to think of that.

She lunged into an immediate attack and almost had her man. He backed away in surprise — directly in front of where Carrana stood.

The portly princess promptly picked up a plate and smashed it over the man's head. It had not enough force to do him serious harm but it certainly did distract their attacker for a moment.

Fachalana lunged in again. The man parried with his right and almost brought the blade in his left through her guard. She would need be attentive of this two-handed assault.

From the corner of her eye, she saw Modareth hurrying his wife from the room. Good, they would be safe. And it was only right that he would think first of Carrana's life.

Back and forth, they attacked and parried. The assassin was skilled. As, after all, he should be, she told herself.

There was shouting. Modi calling for help, she guessed. There were always plenty enough good fellows about here, be they guardsmen or gardeners. They would run to the prince's aid.

The assassin realized this too. He lunged desperately, hoping either to overwhelm her or break by and make his escape. Fachalana saw the opening he left and felt the dagger in her hand and drove it to the hilt into the man's chest.

~ ~ ~

"Do you wish to stay in those same rooms, boy?" asked Borrago. "We could find a larger space for you."

Donzalo considered this quite unexpected question. "It is enough for me, Father. Even if I had more books," he answered.

"Once we marry, Dame Sima and I shall take your grandmother's former chambers." Borrago had insisted upon this title for his lady ever since announcing their engagement. She sat beside him now, as the three took lunch together in the count's tower apartment. "I'll keep my bachelor rooms here, however, for my everyday work."

"But, Donzalo, you need a retinue now. A man-servant, at least. There is no room for anyone but you in that cave of yours."

There came a rap at the door. "That should be Copago. I want his advice on this.

"Come in," he called.

The master of arms entered and nodded respectfully to each in turn. "My lord. Mother. Sir Donzalo."

"Sit, Copago, and fill a plate," said Borrago. "Be sure to have some of these ribs. The new cook is a master of sauces! I have suggested that my son have a retinue and intend to set an allowance upon him." He wiped his fingers after slipping a bone to the dog that lolled beneath the table and looked up at the man. "What think you?"

"I think, sir, that whatever sum you have in mind you should double." His mother laughed aloud at that. Borrago's stinginess was legendary.

The count knew this and chuckled as well. He took some pride in his reputation.

Sir Copago went on, more seriously now. "Much depends on what future we have planned for Donzalo. And what future Donzalo has planned for himself."

All three looked to the young knight. He sighed and began. "Sometimes, I think I would like nothing better than to go back to the Cuddon and live my life out there." Donzalo paused a moment, seemingly lost in memory, before adding, "Our kin would welcome me."

"But you are not yet ready for that, are you?" asked Copago. "I've been talking with Sir Habidros. He has a high opinion of you." Turning to Count Borrago, he continued. "If Donzalo were to have retainers, he could do well to start with Habidros."

"He seems a good man. Not one I would want in my garrison, but well suited to serve in such a role." The count looked straight and steadily at his son. "As competent as you have become, I still want you to have a bodyguard. Guesare may be gone but his brother seems a good stand-in.

"By the way," he said, turning to look at Copago, "what is the other brother up to?"

"He has pitched his tents at the fair, sir, and intends to remain until May Festival."

"Galaro has told me he will ride north then and return for the Summer Fair," spoke Donzalo. "The men of the Cuddon will ride with him on their way home."

"Then we must speak to this Habidros before he decides to ride off with them," said Count Borrago. "Try these fried cakes, Copago. I have never tasted such a mixture of spices!"

~ ~ ~

Lord Doufan's secretary was not a man of Sharsh. He had come from Lorj where he had been trained in that land's scribal tradition. Why he had chosen to come to Sharsh and serve Doufan, perhaps only he and that diplomat knew.

Jobareth Nafal certainly had no idea. Nor, he realized, did he know the man's name. It would seem silly to ask him at this point.

Yet it seemed equally silly to address him simply as 'Scribe,' in the manner of his master. He had avoided the man while they were in the Mountain Keep and now that they were again on the road there would be little interaction. That would probably change when they reached Oles and took river passage down to County Rosam.

And more so when they were settled into the embassy there.

The ambassador had again insisted on a horse litter for his transportation. The way here, however, was far easier going than had been the Royal Road up to the Keep. It sloped gently down into the broad valley of the Weldar, passing over rolling hills and on to the plain.

No one seemed to agree on the name of this highway. Some Sharshites insisted on calling it the Royal Road, maintaining that it was but an extension of that thoroughfare. Others chose to call it the Siphic Road. All agreed that was its name beyond Oles as it passed into the east.

Those who had traveled it the most seemed to settle on Oles Road and so did Jobareth come to refer to it.

He rode now by the side of Lord Doufan's litter. The secretary followed close behind, ready to his master's call, on a donkey. Jobareth understood that this was the traditional steed of a Lorjam scribe.

Where his own little retinue was, he had no idea.

"As you know, Nafal," spoke the ambassador, "Oles is a republic."

"Yes, my lord. As are many of the Siphic cities beyond it."

"True. It is a widespread disease."

"My Lord Doufan disapproves of democracy?" asked the young diplomat.

"Democracy is only the freedom to choose your master," replied Doufan, as ready as ever with an appropriate aphorism. "But these cities are mostly not democracies anyway."

"True indeed, sir. It is the wealthy who rule."

A genuine smile came to Doufan's normally bland countenance. "I am gladdened, Nafal, that I have not been saddled with a dolt on this mission. That would be far too tedious."

He returned to his subject. "Such wealthy men increasingly wield power in our own Sharsh. Your grandfather is one." He glanced up at the younger man. "And you will quite possibly rise to the highest of positions, yourself. I have heard some speak of you as Radal's heir."

Jobareth was unsure of how to respond.

"No, speak not," said Doufan. "Any words would be meaningless. Scribe! Come and read the dispatches to me now."

~ ~ ~

"You do not think I had aught to do with this, Father." It was half a question, half a statement.

"No, Gawis," replied the king. "Do sit down and cease your pacing." Just watching the boy was tiring him. The prince threw himself into one of the deeply cushioned chairs and, as quickly, slid forward to perch on its front edge.

"It's a bad business, sir. I don't know what to think."

"I think we owe much to the Lady Fachalana," said the third person in the room. Prince Gawis turned his eyes toward Lady Lis, who, until now, had been quietly reading. Gawis had no quarrels with the Lady. He did not remember his own mother and much preferred his father's current mistress to his late step-mother.

He had hated the mother of Modareth and Lomela and was certain the emotion had been returned. Lis, the widow of some minor baron, had no agenda and she pleased his father. Would that he could do the same.

"That we do," agreed Lareth. "It was great good fortune that she chose that time to visit." Or was it fortune? the king wondered to himself. There is almost certainly more to it.

"It is true," he went on, "that the would-be assassin was traced to one of your circle, Gawis. What was his name?"

"The assassin or the employer, my lord?" asked Lis, with a little smile. "Lady Fachalana recognized the attacker as a bodyguard of one Godos.

"Yes, Godos. A scion of the Tasetha family." The Tasethas were wealthy merchants and owners of a considerable fleet.

"I am convinced he had no part — the lad has too much money

and too little brain to involve himself. Still, I did suggest to his father that he board one of their ships and voyage elsewhere for a time."

"But some one of my supposed friends is surely involved."

"Surely, indeed." The boy is showing some brains for once, thought his father. "We can always assume that at least one or two of those in a prince's circle are in somebody's employ."

Lareth sighed deeply. "I do fear your father-in-law may have had a hand in this."

"The emperor? Oh, of course." Gawis's previous nerves were giving way to a growing numbness.

"The Partanacans would not like to see Modi sire an heir to challenge your daughters. And the emperor may fear you would be tempted to put aside his daughter in hopes of conceiving a son with some other woman."

The prince nodded. The idea had crossed his mind on occasion.

Lareth guessed as much. "That would be unwise," he said. "Partanaca is too powerful to make an enemy."

"It is hard to be a king, isn't it, Father?" came Gawis's near-whispered reply. "I think I begin to understand the motto on our crest."

"*The king is the servant of the people.* Your grandfather put it there for a reason."

# 4

Lareth's bridge across the Chas had become a favored meeting place for the citizens of Celatas. "I'll see you at King's Bridge," they would say, or "wait for me at the midspan." One could see most of the city from that wooden center span that lay between two great stone piers. One could see far up the broad river, and down as far as the bend below town.

It had also become Ansa's favored place to pass messages along. She had just handed off her last report to her brother. Soon, she and Fachalana should be on the road and out of contact.

Their two-week run of 'The Purloined Pigeon' would be quickly over. It had been easy enough to throw the show together at the last moment. Every actor knew the lines for at least one character in the old warhorse. Those actors would scatter now for the summer, off with touring troops or taking odd jobs around the city until the fall theater season.

She batted a stealthy hand away. The bridge had also become a favored spot for pickpockets and confidence men. "I'll cut it off next time," she whispered and let the would-be thief slip back into the crowd.

Ansa and Fachalana on the road — it sounds like a comedy, she thought, the sort one would fill with mishaps and misadventures. The leads would be two flighty and naïve women — old maids from the country, maybe — taking on the wide world, to roars from the crowd.

But these two women were neither flighty nor naïve. Well, maybe the Lady Fachalana could be on occasion. But she had shown herself to be more than Ansa had ever guessed she might be in her recent encounter with the assassin.

And some might consider them old maids, even. She smiled to herself at that.

Did slaying a man trouble her friend? she then wondered. Ansa had killed and knew it was not something to be done lightly and forgotten.

Ansa looked downriver, toward the docks and warehouses that lined its banks. Sea-going ships did not come this far upriver but the large riverboats were impressive enough. Someday, she would like to board one and go take a look at the sea.

~ ~ ~

"What news I received in the Cuddon did make passing mention of my father's interest in Dame Sima. Finding them engaged when I returned home was unexpected.

"As was," he added, "learning of my grandmother's passing."

"Nafal spent much time with her in her final days," said Sir Blen. "I regret that I really never came to know the Lady Vibola."

"Have you news of Jobareth?" Donzalo asked. "I know he corresponds with Lady Lomela but she has had no time for me."

"The latest rider brought word that he and the ambassador have left Mountain Keep on their journey here. Their diplomatic duties would call for them to arrive in time for the Summer Feast and the count's wedding."

"Seven weeks. That should be enough time, even coming down the river," observed the Laman.

"How like you the new quarters?" asked Blen. "I never saw your old ones but they were described to me."

Donazalo could imagine that description, probably couched in the colorful words of a certain minstrel. "There is more room, for certain. Room enough for Habidros, had he wished, but he preferred to lodge in the barracks, so it is only I and the man-servant that was forced upon me."

"You should have asked instead for a librarian."

"Indeed, yes! I am still in need of bookshelves." Donzalo gestured toward the stacked volumes around the room's perimeter. "It is nice," he added, "to have a window, even if only the one."

"And there is the famous mace," remarked Blen, fixing his eyes on said weapon, temporarily reposing on the mantle. "Yes, I know that story. Such have a way of leaking out."

25

"Probably through the mouth of Guesare," guessed Donzalo, "and well embellished in the telling."

"This Habidros you have taken on is his brother?"

"One of four half-brothers, and of them perhaps the most alike to Guesare." He gave the Sharshite a long look. "I have no doubt you already know all this and of his brother Galaro, as well."

"Ever direct, Sir Donzalo! I like that." He had been toying with his goblet and now raised it to take a sip. Blen had never been a heavy drinker. "And I hope to better understand you." He left his explanation at that.

"Maybe when I understand myself, I can help you," came Donzalo's wry response.

That answer, in itself, helps me, thought Blen. But there was much more to be learned of the plots and secrets that seemed to revolve around this affable young man, this unassuming hero.

"You mistrust me," he said aloud, "yet Jobareth Nafal and I serve the same master. I am no more your enemy than is he." Blen remembered that Lord Radal had once said much the same words to him. That thought momentarily disturbed him.

"That may be so," replied Donzalo, "but neither are you yet my friend."

~ ~ ~

The courier had come at great speed, with a letter directly from the hand of the king. Radal sat by the window in his high tower, the window that looked east toward Lama, and carefully broke the seal.

His henchman Sojel had been waiting when Lord Radal entered Mountain Keep. They had closeted long before he sent the sergeant on his way, to do his bidding and work his will in Lama.

He was gambling with his future, the sorcerer knew, going against the express orders of his king. Radal no longer cared; he wished only to drag Donzalo Rosam down to share in his own damnation.

Ah, but there was his daughter to consider. If only he could teach Fachalana enough, make her sufficiently strong to stand against the

26

world as he had. He knew she had the ability but he could not give her the self-discipline she needed.

They had again made the attempt at a link when he had arrived. The girl was excited about something and that did not help. Radal did glean the fact that there had been an assassination or an attempt at one and that Fachalana was somehow involved. That weighed on him.

Until the courier brought this dispatch. He read it carefully, then read it again. One could rarely, if ever, say that the lord councilor showed delight in anything, but there could be no other description for the look that came to his dark face.

If only Fachalana could bring the skills and discipline she showed in swordplay to bear on her studies of sorcery! No, thought Radal, they are very different endeavors and therein lies the problem. One is about quick decisions and reading situations and the other about the slow and steady imposition of ones will. His daughter was not willing to focus long enough on one thing. She looked to the next challenge, the next riposte and parry.

We will speak on it when she arrives, he told himself. A fortnight or so? He had lost track of the day here.

And we must try to learn what brought her to the door of Modareth at that hour.

~ ~ ~

The keep of Sir Paren had changed little. Corgos saluted the guard who opened the gate to him.

"It is good to have you back, Captain."

"It is good to be back."

His wife would be waiting in their cottage behind the main hall but first he must report to Sir Paren. He wondered if he should mention the news he had heard of Perdos. Once again, that banished knight had come off in a favorable light.

Paren himself came to the door to greet him. "My brother sent word you would soon arrive. Here boy," he said, addressing a groom, "take the Captain's horse and be sure it receives a good rubdown."

Sir Corgos alit from the saddle, somewhat stiffly from his three days travel, and bowed to the reeve. Also stiffly, as Paren duly noted.

"Come on in. I sent a page to tell Tiana you have arrived. You both dine with me and my lady tonight." He stepped back and looked the man over. "Yes, I know you are weary but I want to hear all the news. And then hear it again tomorrow, in more detail!"

It *was* good to be back.

~ ~ ~

Not one, but two bridges span the Weldar at Oles. The burgess of that town, with their love of regulation, decreed that one would serve eastbound traffic and the other, travelers to the west. This naturally confused visitors to the city who ofttimes found themselves needing to turn about and seek the other span.

"My credentials would let us pass no matter which bridge we chose," declared Lord Doufan. "Let us go to the wrong one so I may prove it."

Is this his idea of a jest? wondered Jobareth. It did seem in character for the man. Or perhaps he thought it a way to cow the ruling council of Oles before he ever met them.

"We will go by the proper bridge," said the the caravan-master, and so they did.

"Perhaps it is just as well," Doufan confided to his second-in-command. "If they didn't let us through it would have been most embarrassing." Jobareth Nafal could only nod in agreement and a bit of bewilderment.

The ambassador had abandoned his litter and, for the first time in this journey, sat astride a horse. Doufan knew how to project a proper image, when need be. "We must make three official visits," said he. "First to the council, then to the pontifex, and finally our own embassy here. But unofficially, it would be well to contact our diplomats first. See to it, Nafal, will you?"

Jobareth had already dispatched a man to the embassy but he said nothing of it. He did suspect that Doufan knew.

"The pontifex, sir? The other two I expected."

"Many Lamans consider the Pontifex of Oles to be the head of their religion. It is well to be friendly to him."

"In County Rosam, they mostly defer to their own hierophant — and the wishes of the count — even while giving lip service to the pontifex," Jobareth pointed out.

"We will be friendly to them as well, my boy, even if the southerners are considered to be somewhat schismatic up here."

The younger man shook his head. "Laman politics are bad enough but when we throw in their Kamatian religion, if exceeds understanding."

"That is why I make no effort to understand, Nafal. A smile and a polite word is often all that's needed." Jobareth did not believe him for a moment.

"It is to be noted," continued Lord Doufan, "that our friends in County Arvaram give their allegiance to the pontifex in Lorj, who has claim to being the first and original. Whether they believe he is the true head of their faith or merely wish to oppose the Rosam on yet another issue is anyone's guess."

"I would not be surprised to see my friend Grippo back in County Rosam rise to hierophant one day," said Jobareth, musing more than making a statement.

"A good friend to have then," replied Doufan. "But it is not wise to rely overmuch on such friends."

"Indeed, my lord, indeed."

They had passed into the center of Oles, where much was built of gray granite and the streets were well-paved with cobblestones. Jobareth thought he had never seen so clean a city.

"It is quite hideous, is it not?" asked Lord Doufan.

"Yes, I suppose it is, sir. I would not want to live here."

"Then pray to Jov that you are never named ambassador to Oles." Doufan winked at his younger companion. "The citizens are even worse.

"And this would be the City Hall, where we must greet the Council and, no doubt, an assortment of prominent burgess whom we shall promptly forget. Follow me, Nafal, and then decide if you truly want a life as a diplomat." The ambassador was still chuckling when they passed through the great bronze doors.

## 5

"Farewell, my brother," said Galaro. The two over-sized men, much alike aside from one being bearded and the other clean-shaven, embraced fiercely. "We shall meet again at Summer Feast — if you can bear to stay put that long!"

"I have been both leader and follower," said Habidros. "I can follow young Donzalo for at least a few weeks."

The Cuddonian trader swung up into his saddle. "Let's go, boys! We have a lot of road to follow before we return."

His brother stood a while in the center of the Great Road, watching the troop dwindle into the north. Then he mounted up and started back across Count Borrago's fair ground, already half-empty as more merchants packed up. Today was May Festival and the Spring Fair was at an end.

His young master was at some religious affair, at that open-air temple up above the town. He had noted it in passing, a typical Kamatian stoa. There were some of that religion in the Siphics and it seemed to be spreading.

Habidros was not a religious man. He did, however, carry an assortment of charms to keep him safe. In that, he was not unlike many another soldier.

He pulled out a small silver medal bearing the likeness of the goddess Esefa. This day was special to her; back home they would be wrapping her image in garlands of flowers. He sighed and felt momentarily homesick. Then he shook the reins and headed his steed toward Castle Rosam.

~ ~ ~

Neither Fachalana nor Ansa had ever taken the road to Mountain Keep. Lady Fachalana had simply never had reason to travel there. Ansa, as a spy, had followed more roundabout ways in and out of Sharsh.

"I feel as though I should whisper," said Fachalana, "amid all this beauty. It is like a great temple." She did not whisper but neither did she speak very loudly.

Ansa had seen wonders in her own travels, yet she was inclined to agree. "I fear the Murb does not appreciate it."

Murbalana was the sour middle-aged woman whom Radal had insisted accompany them as chaperon. It would not do for a young noblewoman such as the Lady Fachalana to travel alone. Murbalana complained a great deal, about the food, about the bumpy road, about her husband who had run off some twenty years before.

For the most part, she remained in one of the wagons, where she complained about having no one to complain to. At times, the fourth member of their party, a stolid man-servant to handle the luggage, rode with her. Being deaf, he did not mind the complaints but rather liked the fact that she was talking to him. He imagined that the Mistress Murbalana fancied him somewhat.

But the young women went horseback. Fachalana rode sidesaddle, as would any lady of breeding, and she did it well.

Ansa, feeling freed from her usual need for pretense, had donned Anian trousers and sat astride her mount. This, Murbalana considered the height of scandal. Were it not for her hair, still dyed black from her last role, none would mistake her for anything other than the Ani she was.

Indeed, Fachalana began to wonder if there were more to her friend than she had realized.

The way was growing ever steeper. A fellow traveler, a merchant who passed this way frequently, said they were but two days from the Keep. And then on to Lama!

Fachalana dreamed sometimes of Donzalo in these starry, pine-scented mountain nights. Perhaps Ansa did too.

~ ~ ~

A tiny coffin was consigned to the fire. A woman cried and a man put his arm around her shoulders. A priest spoke a few words of sympathy.

Donzalo watched from the small crowd of relatives. He knew of loss. But then, don't we all, sooner or later? Lomela did not need his presence right now. He would visit in a day or two and things would go on.

Brother Grippo passed by, in procession. Donzalo gave him an unacknowledged nod. Grippo would become a priest this year, wouldn't he?

He put his hand to the silver wolf that was ever present on his shoulder. Yes, we all know loss.

That night, for the first time in nearly a year, Bolos Rosam got drunk.

~ ~ ~

Two long, narrow, flat-bottomed vessels slid down the Weldar's stream. There had been three tedious days crammed with meetings in Oles, and Jobareth Nafal was relieved to at last see that city's docks fade from view.

Lord Doufan, seasoned diplomat that he was, seemed to thrive there. Jobareth had never seen a man so at ease in a crowded room, ever ready with the proper word or expression, soothing where soothing was needed, effortlessly inducing men to speak freely, even of things they should not.

He knew he had better watch himself or he might as easily fall under the ambassador's spell.

In the front of his boat, Pol and Benawis sat conversing. He had been too busy to notice that they had become friends since leaving Mountain Keep. What could the two have in common? Jobareth realized he knew almost nothing of his secretary's background. Most young, low-ranking diplomats came either from the minor nobility or the rising middle class.

Pol, of course, was of the peasantry. Wasn't he? The legate realized he didn't really know him very well either. The young fellow's accent suggested that he came from the north, perhaps even Arolin.

One of the men at arms had informed him that the pair spent most of their free time in Oles visiting the brothels. Jobareth could hardly censure that — he had on occasion frequented such establishments himself in his student days. Whores held little interest now for him.

Jobareth Nafal knew the one woman he wanted and he knew she would remain always beyond his reach. Yet in a few weeks he would be seeing her.

As well as the woman he could well end up marrying. It might be the only way to get the Lady Fachalana away from her father's influence. That would be a good thing, wouldn't it?

Jobareth felt sure he could convince himself it was.

## 6

Things would be different this time, Sojel assured himself.

He did not hurry as he rode south by circuitous ways but roughly paralleling the west bank of the Weldar. It would be necessary to reform his band when he reached his destination. Not so many now and just the best men.

It would not do to linger in Count Dordos's lands. They lay too close to County Rosam, too vulnerable to being spied upon. No, he would take the men south and cross the river a few at a time, here and there, so as not to arouse suspicion.

He wondered for a moment what had happened to his former second-in-command, Vanob. Sojel was not one to dwell on such things for long; still, it was odd that Van had never showed up.

He would have been a good man for the work at hand, thought Sojel. As it is, I may just have to do it all myself.

Sojel did rather like that idea.

~ ~ ~

"Your friend already knows most of your secrets, doesn't she? More of them, perhaps, than you realize."

Lord Radal had insisted that his daughter's companion accompany her to his chambers. This made Ansa understandably apprehensive. She had heard much of Fachalana's father yet had never met him.

What does he know? wondered Ansa. She felt suddenly trapped.

"Yes, Father," replied Fachalana, baffled – and intrigued – by the seeming tension between the two. "There is nothing we need hide from Maresta."

Radal looked long at the young spy and then shrugged. "I am sure whatever matters I would speak of here to you would sooner or later reach her ears. So stay, my lady."

The sorcerer had wondered about his daughter's comrade for some time. She did look Anian, didn't she?

He turned his gaze back to his daughter. "You are become the heroine of all Celatas. I have little doubt that the king will bestow some title on you, with income to match." He smiled thinly. "Perhaps I won't need to give you so large an allowance now."

Ansa managed a small smile as well. Lord Radal did not seem nearly so terrifying as his reputation had him.

She knew, however, not to be fooled.

"I am proud of you too, my dear," he told his daughter and truly meant it. "But a question remains: why did you go to Prince Modareth's house on that day and at that hour?"

"I — I had dreams, Father. I heard a voice, a far-away voice. I know not what it said but I awoke knowing Modi, I mean Prince Modareth, was in trouble.

"I *had* to go."

The Lord Councilor thought on this a moment. "That was the night we tried to speak to each other, wasn't it?"

"Yes, sir." Fachalana glanced toward her friend. "Maresta doesn't really know much about that. I suppose I may have, um, mentioned the idea in passing."

"The wizard-link is no secret, my girl, though most do not under-stand how it works." He fixed his eyes again upon the Anian. "And unless one has talent, it makes no difference how much one knows. This one," he said, giving a nod toward Ansa, "does not."

For which I give thanks, said Ansa to herself.

"So," the dark sorcerer continued, "I can guess what occurred."

"Was it a god?" asked his daughter. She still had hopes.

"Nay, Fachalana." Her father could not help laughing outright this time, nor could Ansa help joining him. "I believe it was another wizard, speaking to someone else. Someone who was arranging an assassination attempt.

"You must never have completely left your link and somehow ended up overhearing them. That," he said with sudden gravity, "takes great ability. I know of only two sorcerers, mighty mages, who have reputedly done so.

"Ah, if only you could harness such a talent and do it at will."

Ansa decided to speak up. Why not, after all? "Who, my lord, would have been planning such an attack?"

Radal shook his head. "There are too many possibilities. The link does not require great natural capability and many can enter it. You, too, will in time," he said to his daughter. "It is in you.

"There is much in you, Fachalana, and you have yet to discover it."

He rose and went to a narrow window. They had met in a lower room of Radal's tower, a tower only he and those he invited ever entered. Higher up were the chambers where he practiced his magics, where folks saw strange lights playing in the night.

This room held only an ordinary desk and chairs.

"Come to the window," said Lord Radal. "One can see Lama from here."

Fachalana peered through the opening. "It looks just like Sharsh," said she.

"That it does," replied her father. "I still have my reservations about allowing this. Take care, Fachalana, on the road and at Castle Rosam.

"And I charge you, Maresta, with keeping her from getting into trouble."

All three knew that might prove a difficult task.

~ ~ ~

Galaro stood in his stirrups and looked up the road. "I would recognize that rider anywhere," said he.

"An enemy or a friend?" asked the man who rode beside him. He cocked his head so he might regard his captain with his one good eye.

"A brother."

"Ah, then both."

"You must have brothers," remarked Galaro. He raised a hand in greeting as the horseman came nearer.

"Have you come to play us a song, Brother?" he roared.

"I might as well serenade the deaf!" came the answer. Then both men were off their steeds and, after only a moment's hesitation, embraced.

"Friends, it seems," remarked Galaro's companion.

"Nay, Guesare hates my guts. And with good reason!" He held his half-brother at arms' length and spoke. "I would hope you might forgive some of what I did to you as a lad."

"Some," agreed the minstrel.

"'Tis better than none," allowed Galaro, "nor do I expect you to forget what has been. Are you on your way to Castle Rosam?"

"That I am."

"You need not hurry. Your young friend is in good hands. Those of our brother Habidros, in fact." The burly trader turned to his train of followers. "There is a good spot to pitch our tents a half-league up the road," he called to them. "Let us do so.

"And I would that you stay with us tonight, Guesare. You may even play your rebec, if you don't mind the accompaniment of good Cuddonian bagpipes."

"I thought I had escaped those! But I will encamp with you this night, Brother," said the minstrel, vaulting onto his wiry pony.

Guesare admired the efficiency with which the troop set up their tents on a field bordering a middling-sized village. Potential buyers began to show up immediately.

"We will not do much business here," confided Galaro, "but there is no point in bypassing a sales opportunity. And, after all, we do need to stop and sleep somewhere.

"These necklaces come directly from Lorj," he said to a woman who was perusing his wares. Guesare doubted that the villager believed Galaro's sales pitch but, knowing him to be a smuggler, thought it might well be true.

As they relaxed by the fire that night, Guesare idly strumming his rebec, the brothers filled each other in on recent events.

"It seems I should thank you for saving Donzalo's life," said Guesare.

"Possibly. Habi and Sir Corgos are competent fighters, They might have gotten him to safety on their own." The two sat without speaking for a few minutes.

"Your old acquaintance Perdos rode with me a while in the spring," spoke Galaro of a sudden.

"I assume he still wishes me ill."

"Oh, indeed. One thing that seems most certain, though, is that he is not in league with those who wish to harm Donzalo."

He paused, composing his words. "But be careful of the man. We parted ways north of Ros-town and I suspect he yet lurks about those parts." He turned to Guesare. "Why don't you ride north with us? We will return to Count Borrago's lands for the Summer Fair."

"You fear for me on the road?" Guesare was surprised that his long-estranged brother would feel concern for him. Or maybe he thinks to make up for our past, he thought.

No, he could not postpone his return to Castle Rosam a month or more. Too much was coming together there and he needed to be in place before it did.

"I must decline, my brother. I shall see you at Summer Feast."

~ ~ ~

"I was once ambassador in Morparas, you know," remarked Lord Doufan for no particular reason, as they watched the fog-shrouded river banks slide by. Or no reason that Jobareth could discern. One could be sure of nothing with the ambassador.

At any rate, Jobareth did know this. He had learned all he could of the man before they left Sharsh.

"Is it like to Oles, sir?" he asked.

Doufan laughed loudly. "There are no two cities more unalike! Morparas is dirty and dangerous and disorganized. It was also the largest city I had ever seen. Larger than any in Sharsh, though no city in Lama proper rivals Celatas."

"I was told that Lanlaz dwarfs even Morparas." This he had heard from Guesare, the only man he personally knew — until he met Doufan's scribe — who had been to the isle of Lorj.

"Some say it is the largest city in the world." Doufan looked up as the boatswain approached.

"This be a dangerous stretch of the river, gentlemen," he said. "Best keep a watch out for pirates and such."

"As long as it is not one of my former wives, I shall feel safe," said Lord Doufan.

The man chuckled appropriately and went aft to speak to the other passengers on deck. Most chose to remain in the open air in this warm weather, rather than the stuffy cabin that sat midship. The increasing swarms of biting insects were beginning to change some minds.

They danced above the water, swarming in the misted golden light of morn. It was growing warmer. Jobareth came near to dozing off.

Then he spied a pair of skiffs, partly concealed in the willows overhanging the stream. They were filled with men.

"Guardsmen! To arms!"

Immediately, each man at arms rose in his place, hand to his sword, as did Jobareth. The ruffians in the boats stayed where they were and only glared at the travelers as they passed.

Doufan eyed him appraisingly. "You are a good man to have about in a crisis, Nafal. Have you ever considered a career in the military rather than diplomacy?"

~ ~ ~

"No, I'll not drink, Jak."

Bolos waited while the sergeant of his guard quaffed his tankard of ale. He found himself watching how the lamplight reflected from the man's bald head. Could I be losing my hair? he wondered. His father, the count, had been bald nearly as long as he could remember.

The stolid soldier wiped his beard on the back of his hand and looked at his master. "You shouldn't beat yourself up over it, sir, if I may say so. 'Twas only once."

Bolos nodded without speaking.

"And you've done well this past year," continued Sir Jak. "The boys are all pulling for you, sir."

"This past year has not done well by me." Jak recognized the self-pity in his employer's words but felt maybe the man had a right to it. It was not to him to judge, anyway.

"Is there anything I should know about?" asked Bolos, breaking the silence that had followed his plaint. Jak was relieved. Now they could get down to business.

"Not really, my lord. Your father still visits the house of Sir Copago more evenings than not. And when he does, he usually stays the night."

"What of my brother? Donzalo." Bolos did not want the man to think he meant his half-brother Copago or that he even acknowledged their kinship.

He had received a letter from the king's councilor, Lord Radal, stating that Sharsh had his interests in mind and warning him against the ambitions of Count Orgelo. This had served to strengthen the suspicions he already had.

Should he trust Radal? He still did not understand why he and the king had tried to kill his brother. But the message also suggested he keep an eye on Donzalo. It was not an accusation but it made Bolos wonder.

"He has kept to himself, sir, for the most part. I set a man to watch him but he finds little to report." The burly soldier chuckled. "It seems he spends the better part of his time sorting his library."

"Keep up the watch." Sir Bolos sighed. "Whatever is coming, we must be ready for it."

## 7

"Sharshite nobles may not haggle but it is expected in Lama," explained Ansa. She held up two fingers to the roadside fruit merchant. He nodded his agreement, handing over slices of melon in exchange for a pair of copper coins.

"All of us," she told the man. "Don't try to cheat me."

Their entourage had grown. Lord Radal had insisted that two guardsmen be added, making the group now six strong. Ansa had been glad of those two men at arms when they spied a band of men in the distance, cutting across their path. She breathed easier when the troop continued toward the south on whatever business it had.

"Mercenaries, I would wager, my lady," whispered one of the guards. Ansa nodded her agreement.

The purveyor of melons distributed his ware to all, the two soldiers on their horses, Murbalana and the man-servant in a two-wheeled cart. The deaf servant, known only as Doo — but who did not answer to any name — enjoyed being in charge of driving the wagon and was sure that Mistress Murbalana admired his skill.

She seemed to comment on it frequently.

They had turned from the Oles Road and now traveled south-easterly toward County Rosam. This was the route the couriers of Sharsh usually took.

"You were certainly right about Lama being hot," said Fachalana.

"Wait a month," replied her companion. Though she knew better than to wear an Ani costume in Lama, Ansa still straddled her mount. The Lady Fachalana noticed that it was not uncommon for women of the countryside to do so here.

She also continued to dye her hair.

Ansa daydreamed sometimes about meeting Donzalo again. Would he recognize her with her dark tresses, now cut shorter than when he had known her? Would the clothes of a gentlewoman rather than a serving maid fool him?

Would he remember her at all?

There was also the possibility that Borrago would have her thrown into a cell as a spy as soon as she set foot on his lands.

"How far to the next inn?" she asked the Laman.

"If you are not too picky, my lady, less than a league," replied the fellow.

To Fachalana, he looked a typical peasant of the land, slight, olive-skinned and dark haired. She had to admit that they all seemed much alike to her.

Her friend had taken charge of their little company. She knew Maresta was competent but this surprised her. Fachalana was accustomed to being the leader in any circle she entered.

The Lady Fachalana was more suspicious than ever that the actress was not all she seemed.

~ ~ ~

"I want you to remain in the keep for a while longer," said the King of Sharsh to his younger son, "and I want you to remain guarded."

Modareth nodded. He turned to his wife and took her hand. "Whatever you think best, Father." As soon as the two had seated themselves before the king's desk, Modareth had slid his chair close to that of his wife.

"Sire," spoke the Princess Carrana, somewhat hesitantly. "Do — do you think the Lady Fachalana might be named my lady-in-waiting?"

Lareth liked it immediately. "Yes, my dear, an excellent idea. It would give her an official position at the court — just what she needs when I make her a viscountess." He smiled at how the pair looked to each other at that. "You realize that she would no doubt be very lax in her duties."

"She has attended her duties very well, sir," said Modareth. "I would certainly not complain."

"Perhaps I should also name her your bodyguard," jested the king. "But you are correct, my boy. Fachalana has already served us as well as any person might. If she never lifted another finger for us, we would still be satisfied with her.

"Now, we must speak of you and your bride and who might seek to kill you."

"It is about the succession, isn't it, sir?"

"Almost certainly," said Lareth, "and, therefor, it shall continue to be a problem. Partanaca may be behind it. Or it may be some sycophant of your brother who thinks to better secure his place."

"You think the former, don't you Father?"

"Yes, Modi, I do." Why couldn't Gawis have half the brains of this one? wondered King Lareth. When it comes time, I hope the older brother has sense enough to lean on the younger.

"Would we be safer in the country, sir?" asked Carrana. She wasn't exactly dim-witted either, was she?

"Maybe. A well-defended keep somewhere might be ideal. Not too far from here, of course, and near a garrison."

He looked at the pair and was a bit surprised by the fondness he felt for them, fondness he had always seemed to reserve for Modareth's siblings. "For now, however, remain safe here in my fortress. And maybe make me a grandson so we can truly worry the Partanacans!"

The king laughed to see both blush so deeply.

~ ~ ~

"You have fallen in the world, Hendel of Pora."

The stout cook looked up at the mention of his name. "Thanks to you and your master." He nearly spat out his reply.

Sojel barked a derisive laugh. "No one forced Sharsh's silver into your hand."

Two of his henchmen stood behind him in the tavern doorway. They were the last that he needed to get across the river, here at Todmouth.

All the way down the Weldar, he had kept his men to their task, not allowing them to turn aside for plunder or sport, sending two or three across at a time, with orders to meet up later. Most should be waiting for him when he crossed.

"You know these scoundrels?" asked the woman behind the bar.

She was not a young woman nor was she pleasant to look upon. But Mistress Oba owned this tavern and here she was a queen.

She had her own henchmen should any be unwilling to recognize her as such.

Hendel turned toward his employer. "I knew Sergeant Sojel when I worked upriver, ma'am. The other two are strangers to me." The cook retained the manners he had learned while serving aristocrats. It had stood him in good stead when he sought a job here.

And, as had others before her, Oba fell in love with his pastries. It was rumored that he was a confection she sometimes sampled as well.

"Humph. If you plan to drink, come in and stop dawdling at the door, boys. If you want food, Hendel is at your service. If you want more than food," she added with a wink, "the girls upstairs can accommodate you."

Hendel shuddered involuntarily at the thought of those 'girls.' They made Mistress Oba look a beauty in comparison.

Sojel and his men seated themselves at a stained and splintered table, the veteran of many a spilled beer and idler's knife. "Ale for us all," he ordered, "and tell the girls to expect us later."

"That I will, sir," said Oba, a smile splitting her leathery face. "That I will."

~ ~ ~

At this early hour, the cliffs below Keep Rosam stood yet in darkness and the sun hid behind its battlements. Guesare gazed upward at their silhouetted shapes for a little while, recalling his memories of the place. Perhaps, next to Drolwym, it was the place most like a home to him.

He recalled an old song of his homeland and spoke the words lowly to himself:

*Travelers all, we wear*
*the dust of yesterday.*
*The rain will fall at last,*
*and gently wash away*
*each fragment of the past,*
*the long road's clinging clay.*
*Travelers all, we fare*
*yet upon our way.*

Ever a traveler — was there any other life for him? He turned his mount toward the winding road up to the castle.

~ ~ ~

They still might not be counted friends, but Sir Blen and Sir Donzalo found themselves spending more time together. Where they spent much of this time was on the green between Castle Rosam's outer walls, exercising their knightly skills.

At times they were joined by Habidros the Cuddonian, now Donzalo's bodyguard. At others, Sir Copago joined them. His duties often had him elsewhere and Habidros did not like to rise early so, frequently, it was only the two. Blen would ride up from the new embassy at dawn — it was a much shorter trip than the one from town — and Donzalo would be there to greet him.

They fenced a great deal. Blen knew he lacked in this skill and that the lanky Laman had become a fine swordsman. He could learn from the boy and about the boy at once.

This morning, he was become somewhat miffed at that boy. With his long arms, Donzalo was choosing to play with him, reaching in and poking him here and there at will with his wooden practice sword. Blen hoped he would never have to face the lad in a real duel!

Suddenly, Donzalo dropped his guard and stared at something behind Blen.

"That would have been a great mistake in combat," came a voice. "Sir Blen would have skewered you properly.'

"Guesare!"

Blen turned to see the Cuddonian minstrel astride his pony and held up a hand in greeting. "Welcome back, Sir Guesare."

The man dismounted and took his hand. "It is good to see you, Sir Blen." But he embraced Donzalo as he would a brother.

"Habi should have come down with me," said Donzalo. "He has missed the opportunity to greet you in exchange for an extra hour of sleep."

"He probably considers it a fair bargain," remarked Guesare. "I hear he is now your man."

Donzalo nodded. "You are leaving, Blen?"

"Back to my duties, Donni," the knight replied, as he tied his gear to his horse's saddle. "Tomorrow?"

"I shall await you. And trounce you once again."

"Undoubtedly," laughed the Sharshite as he swung a leg over his steed and headed for the gates.

When did these two become friends? wondered Guesare, waiting while Donzalo gathered up his own gear.

## 8

The shores of the Weldar grew ever more populated. There were many villages now and farm fields that ran right down to the water's edge. This was the rich middle of the great river valley, and the counts who ruled it were wealthy men.

The wealthiest of these was Borrago, Count Rosam. They were only two days from Ros-town now, the boatswain told the Sharshites.

Sometimes the Great Road swung close to the river and they watched the traffic upon it, lone riders and men afoot, farmers' wains, bands of merchants. At first, more seemed to travel north, back the way they had come; now, traffic seemed more balanced, with many heading toward the south, toward County Rosam.

"They're starting to come back this way for the Summer Fair," said Pol.

Doufan seemed subdued as he surveyed the richness of the countryside they passed. "I never quite understood why the king attached such importance to this embassy," he confided to Nafal. "Now, I think I do."

"Lord Radal considers the Lamans dangerous," said Jobareth in return. He remembered when he had first come to Keep Rosam, as the dark sorcerer's aide.

"Lord Radal is frightened of many things."

"Indeed? He does not seem so."

"He puts on a good front but Radal is an empty man. Despair walks ever at his side and Death close behind." Lord Doufan smiled at his young compatriot's expression. "I rarely wax so poetic. That is your strength, isn't it, Jobareth Nafal?"

It was, thought Jobareth. How long had it been since he wrote anything?

He took a close look at the diplomat, the bland face, the thinning hair. It was so easy to dismiss such a man, to not see him at all.

"Ambassador," he said, "I wonder if Lord Radal might not consider you dangerous as well."

Both sat and watched the shore slide by.

~ ~ ~

"It is even wider than the Chas!" exclaimed Fachalana.

Ansa nodded absently. "The Siph is larger," she said. Then, thinking better of it, added, "Or so I have heard." There was no reason anyone here should know she had ever looked upon the mighty River Siph. Aye, and crossed it more than once.

Right now, they must cross this flow. She motioned for Doo to bring the cart up.

"There should be a ferry," said Ansa, surveying the town spread below them, most of it close to the river banks. The party stood atop a small hill. Across the Weldar they could see Ros-town proper and, above it, Borrago's keep.

Fachalana pointed. "Could that be it on the far side?"

"I believe so," replied the Anian, shielding her eyes from the morning sun. "The count only allows one ferry to operate. Of course, he owns it. If there were but one or two of us, we could find a boatman to take us across but I suppose we shall have to use the official transport." She had employed such boatmen on her previous visit to County Rosam.

"It may be on this side by the time we make it to the river. Let's head down."

Fachalana rode close to her friend and whispered, "From here on I had best play leader of our group. I know you do not want to call attention to yourself."

Ansa agreed. "I can fill the role of demure companion to a great lady. Our looks would make most think us such, anyway."

The Lady Fachalana laughed at that. "Shall I play my part with great haughtiness or am I the sort to treat my underlings well?"

"You have had a lifetime to practice the role, my lady. I think you will find the proper approach.

"Do you wish to present yourself immediately at the count's court?"

"Oh, no, Maresta. Let us find the embassy first. Do you think Jobo might be here yet?"

Their road had become a rutted street lined with shabby wooden structures, mostly warehouses from the look of them.

Ansa shrugged. "We shall find out, soon enough."

There was a capacious dock at the end of their way. Out on the river, the wide, flat-bottomed ferry was slowly steering toward them, oarsmen at a pair of sweeps on either side.

The heart of each beat a little quicker as it approached. Within these two accomplished women there remained yet a pair of impetuous, romantic girls, wondering what great adventure might await them here.

Doo wondered only if Mistress Murbalana would be seduced from his side by the sophisticated men of this city.

~ ~ ~

"It is hard to believe you met Galaro on the road yet you are both still alive."

"Our brother is now a leader of men. I think that changes one." Guesare looked about him. "I like your new digs, Donni."

Donzalo's quarters had more and more come to resemble his old ones. The biggest difference was the large table in the center of this room, overflowing with scraps of manuscript and bit and pieces of mechanical devices. The minstrel walked over and surveyed them. "Cannons, Donzalo?"

"He keeps talking about building a foundry," said Habidros. "'Tis not a bad idea, I think."

Guesare nodded. "Borrago needs more artillery here, whether he buy it or cast it himself. I believe he does not realize how quickly a bombard or two might level this keep."

"We should have emplacements on the river, too," declared Donzalo. "Then we would truly control it."

"You'll never convince the count of that. He's not even convinced his men should have muskets. Yes," continued Habidros, "I have noticed things in my short time here."

"You're the only true soldier of we three, Habi," said his brother. "Donzalo may have need of such, one of these days."

50

"Not if I end up as Uncle Paren's heir. I suspect Habidros would not want to spend the rest of his days serving a rural reeve."

"There are worse fates," opined Guesare. "But we both expect more for you."

Donzalo sighed deeply and, perhaps, with a note of exasperation. "Not the destiny thing again."

"We all have destinies, my boy. Mine is to starve if we don't get down to the kitchens."

~ ~ ~

"Whence came these horses?"

"Which ones, sir?" The little innkeeper looked up at Sojel and then at the knot of armed men behind him.

"That one. And that one over there."

"Oh." He had suspected the soldier meant those ones and also suspected this was not a good thing. "I bought them from a traveling knight. A Sir Perdos. I can give you a good deal on them." Would that he had managed to sell all of them already.

"Isn't that Vanob's mount?" asked one of the men. Sojel ignored him.

"Perdos, you say? Where is this Perdos now?"

"He crossed the river a season ago, having wintered with us. He seemed a good enough fellow."

"A traitor and a deserter is what he is. A murderer of his comrades too, it seems. And you harbored him." Sojel felt his anger as a fire rising within him. He did not tamp it down as he might usually but let his temper rage. He had been frustrated too much and too frequently lately.

He rode his horse into the little man, knocking him down. The innkeeper's wife ran shrieking from the doorway where she had been standing.

Sojel let his warhorse thoroughly trample the body beneath its steel-shod hooves. Before the now-widow could reach her husband's remains, he grasped her by her collar and threw her to the ground before his troop.

"You may have the woman," Sojel told his followers, already eagerly dismounting.

"Bring me a flame!" he shouted, and one of the bravos ran into the inn to return with a lit lantern. Sojel tossed it onto the thatched roof and saw that it readily caught fire.

Two lightly equipped guardsmen had come running up from their post at the ferry. On discovering the number and arms of their opponents they hesitated, then ran the opposite way. Sojel's men easily rode them down.

The sergeant sat in his saddle, satisfied, and watched the inn burn. "Get the horses," he ordered, "and let's be on our way."

## 9

The house was empty. They had been assured that the embassy was at this address.

An idler watched them a while from the shade of an awning across the street, before ambling over. "Looking for the Sharshites? They moved to their new place."

Fachalana sighed wearily. "Thank you, my good man," she said in her most refined tones, playing the role of great lady to the hilt. "Could you tell me where that is?"

The man looked at her slyly. "I could guide you."

Ansa whispered to her friend. "He means for a price." She knew Fachalana might not readily recognize that sort of thing.

The noblewoman said nothing but immediately urged her horse up the street. Ansa signaled for Doo to follow.

"We'll find someone else to point out the road," declared Fachalana.

Which they did and soon found themselves passing out of town and into the hilly countryside. "We could still take rooms in Rostown," said Ansa. "It might be less bother."

"I don't want to waste any more time," replied her friend.

In town, they had learned that Jobareth Nafal and the new ambassador were not yet arrived. They heard quite a bit of news, in fact, on the ferry, at the docks. Lamans, like most folk the world around, enjoyed their gossip. So Ansa and Fachalana were well filled in on the goings-on at Keep Rosam.

They had to ask directions but one more time before they spied a large edifice, obviously still under construction, on a hill to the left of their road. The duo would have made far better time had they not needed to match their pace to that of the cart that followed them.

Murbalana could be heard voicing displeasure over something. They could not make out exactly what and remained as ignorant as the man seated by her.

The ugly, squarish, crenelated building stood in three stories of pinkish stone, the lowest being sunk partly into the ground. "It looks like a fortress," observed Ansa. Sir Blen had a hand in its design, no doubt. "Stay here," she called to the wagon and then held up her palm so Doo would actually know what she meant. The two women rode up the rise toward the embassy.

"I hope they plan to pave this eventually," remarked Fachalana. The ground was rough and rutted from the many wagons that had brought stone and timber up this hill.

"Why, it is Blen himself," whispered Ansa to her comrade, as a man stepped from the wide doorway opening into the basement floor and walked toward them.

"My greetings and welcome to you, Lady Fachalana," said he. "My man in town sent a message saying you had arrived. It came to my hand only moments before you yourself came to my door or I would have ridden down to escort you."

He looked quizzically at Ansa. "Posena?" he said, in sudden recognition. He turned back to the Sharshite noblewoman. "Do you know who this woman is?"

"Be not concerned about it, sir," she replied, slipping down from her mount. "Maresta came here before under my orders and as my agent."

Sir Blen considered her words for a moment. "That clears some things up, my lady," he calmly replied.

He has a cool head on him, thought Ansa. I like that. "Shall I have the cart come up, sir?"

Blen motioned to a pair of men who stood near. "Go fetch up the luggage and see to the servants. You, my ladies, must come in and throw off your road weariness. Maresta, you say?" he asked, helping the young woman dismount. "Is that how we should call you here?"

"Yes," Fachalana said. "Although I have long suspected that too is a made-up name for the stage."

Close to the truth, my friend, thought Ansa.

The knight tossed the reins to a waiting groom and escorted the duo up a wooden stairway — obviously temporary — to the second level and what was clearly intended to be the main entrance. A pair of heavy oak doors hung open.

"It looks better inside than out, my ladies," said Blen. "Would you like to go to your rooms first?"

"I'm starving," stated Fachalana.

Ansa laughed at her friend's directness. "As am I, Sir Blen."

"Then let us lunch together, " said Blen, "and you can tell me all about your trip.

"And maybe," he added, "something about this Maresta whom I knew as Posena the chambermaid."

~ ~ ~

Little Ros was shy of his very large 'Uncle' Donzalo. He had been far too young when last the man who was truly his father had seen or held him and there were no memories.

He hid behind his mother's chair.

"He walks very well for his age," remarked Guesare. The boy was not altogether sure about him either.

"I have heard that Donzalo was the same," replied Lady Lomela. She did not know that the minstrel was privy to the secret of Ros's paternity.

Guesare could see his friend's heart was breaking. Maybe he should never have returned to his home. Maybe a peaceful life in the Cuddon was the only destiny he needed.

Mistress Traspa picked up the toddler. "Nap time, my little lord," said she and carried him to his nursery.

A rap came at the door, to be answered by a chambermaid in Traspa's absence. She admitted a man in robes of white.

"Brother Grippo," said Lomela. "Come in and visit with us."

"Thank you, my lady." He held out a folded paper to her. "A message came from Sir Blen and I offered to deliver it to you."

The princess read the note quickly. "Fachalana is here!" she beamed. "At last! Oh, how I wish that Jobareth had already arrived."

Guesare and Donzalo exchanged thoughtful looks. The name Fachalana meant many things to them, different things to each.

"Is she coming here, my lady?" asked Donzalo.

"Tomorrow morning. Sir Blen will bring her up. Oh, you must meet her, Donni, and you too, Guesare." She laughed. "And Brother Grippo. All of you are always welcome here."

Grippo spoke. "I understand that she is — engaged to our friend Nafal?"

"No, not officially," replied Lomela. "But everyone expects it to be only a matter of time." Once again the other two men exchanged glances.

On their way back to Donzalo's rooms, Guesare warned, "Do not make the mistake of looking for Jola in this woman."

"I know not to, my friend. How do you feel about meeting a sister you never knew you had?"

"Stepsister," Guesare corrected him. "But I, too, must avoid seeing Jola in she who is her sister."

~ ~ ~

"Lord Radal's daughter is here, my lord," said Copago, entering the count's tower study.

Borrago turned to him. "At the castle?"

"No, sir. She is staying in the Sharshite embassy. Sir Blen asks to bring her by tomorrow morning."

"Hmm, what's her name again?"

"Fachalana, my lord. The Lady Fachalana."

"Of course, of course. I don't know how many times Lomela has mentioned it to me." The count shrugged. "Well, let her come."

"Sir." There was concern in his master of arms' voice.

"Speak."

"Her father did try to kill Donzalo. Should we let the two of them, well, be anywhere near each other?"

"You do not think she is an assassin?"

"No, though I have heard some surprising things about her, sir. You heard the story of her saving King Lareth's son from an attack?"

"That was this girl?" Borrago whistled. "I wish I had a better memory for names!" He thought a moment. "Tell Donzalo that I

56

want his man Habidros with him at all times. Most times, anyway. And it wouldn't hurt if his brother Guesare tagged along."

Copago smiled. "That should keep the boy safe."

"We are never safe from women, my lad. Of that you may be sure."

~ ~ ~

"I should not go with you. Not until the Legate arrives."

"Oh, don't call him that, Maresta. He is our friend Jobareth. You could even address him as Jobo and get away with it."

"However I might name him, I want him there to vouch for me before I enter Borrago's keep. You may have prestige in Sharsh but the count does not know you. Nor does he have any love for your father."

"I suppose you are right," admitted Fachalana. "You are always the level-headed one of us." She smiled warmly at her friend. This trip had brought them closer than ever before, had let them become the true equals that true friends must be. "I envy you the extra time to rest while I must be once more on horseback. I don't know if I'll ever be able to sit properly again!"

With that, Fachalana bustled out the door, not to return until late in the day.

Ansa looked about the room for a moment, wondering if she should indeed return to her own and get some extra sleep. No, she was too on edge for that. She would like to see more of the embassy and the countryside that lay around it and she should check in on their traveling companions, too.

The Murb's little chamber was right down the hall, where Ansa and Fachalana could call on her at need. They had no need and no desire to do so, but had let the Sharshites put her where they wished. She rapped lightly on the door. If the woman were asleep, it would be unwise to wake her and provide yet another grievance.

No reply. But what was that thumping noise? She carefully pushed open the unlocked portal to glimpse Murbalana and Doo quite occupied with their own business. As quickly and as quietly as she could, she shut it, her expression hovering somewhere between a smile and a grimace.

Well, at least I need not worry about those two, she told herself. And though her rear end was as sore as Fachalana's, she thought maybe a ride would be a pleasant morning's diversion.

~ ~ ~

"Now you two must be our surrogates while we are gone," said Sir Paren. Corgos and Tiana stood respectfully, waiting for the reeve to mount up.

"Do hurry, my dear," called Lady Thara from one of two wagons. "We are going to travel slowly enough with all this baggage. Do you want to miss your own brother's wedding?"

A half-dozen men at arms sat their horses, waiting, and there were servants and drivers with the wains.

"Very well, my lady," Paren called back to her. "Expect us to be gone at least three weeks, maybe a month," he said. He had told this to his master of arms several times already but thought it bore repeating. "With any luck, maybe we can bring Donni back with us."

"He is a fine young man," replied Captain Corgos. "I would gladly ride with him again."

"It is my hope that neither of you ever has to ride anywhere again," said Sir Paren, mounting up. "No further than my brother's keep, anyway."

He signaled his followers to form up their column and set off down the road toward Keep Rosam.

"Shall I address you as Lady Tiana for the next month?" teased Corgos.

"It wouldn't hurt," replied his bride.

## 10

That had gone well enough, thought the Lady Fachalana.

Borrago had been polite, if a bit brusque, and seemed to bear her no ill will. She was surprised at how short the man was, knowing of his tall son. Fachalana suspected that if she and the count stood side by side, her height would be the greater, and perhaps by more than just a bit.

So much for the official presentation. Now Sir Blen led the way to the Lady Lomela's apartments. The keep was not large by the standards of some she had seen in Sharsh and had a sense of the rustic about it. But it seemed spacious and probably was a comfortable enough place to dwell. It might not be her father's palace but the princess was not suffering here.

Would Donzalo be there? Their meeting would be complicated. This she knew.

And here they were. Ah, Lomela, it has been too long. Is that your little boy? And Traspa! Fachalana entered the room wordlessly and embraced her childhood friend.

There were tears in at least three sets of eyes.

"My ladies," spoke Blen. They turned to look at him, still standing in the doorway. "I will leave you for a little while but return later." Both knew he meant that he would bring guests with him.

There was much to talk about, once their tearful greeting was out of the way. The two sat on Lomela's divan and spoke of many things, Jobareth Nafal being high on the list.

Little Ros stood a while, silently regarding this stranger, and then climbed onto Fachalana's lap. She had never before had a child sit in her lap.

It was not unpleasant.

So it was that Sir Blen found them on his return. With him were three men, two quite large, one of a more ordinary size. From the rebec he carried, Fachalana recognized that the latter was a minstrel and therefor was able to put a name to him: Guesare.

Brother to Donzalo's slain love. A love who was also her own sister.

The two larger fellows looked rather alike, but she had no trouble knowing which was Donzalo. Had she not seen him often enough in dream? The other whispered something in the young knight's ear and then took up a station outside the door. A bodyguard, she surmised.

"Habi is taking his duties too seriously," said Donzalo. "He too is a kinsman but says he will stand guard outside."

Lomela rose from her place. Fachalana was uncertain what to do with the boy in her lap. She gingerly lifted him onto the cushions beside her and came to stand beside the princess.

"This is my old friend, the Lady Fachalana," Lomela said.

"Not old, you silly," broke in Fachalana. The men smiled, which had been her intention, and she smiled back. She knew how to act the role of flirtatious girl. It was a stock character of the stage.

"Very well, Fachalana," replied Lomela, with a laugh that over-flowed with her happiness. There had been few such for a long time. "These are my dear friends Sir Guesare and Sir Donzalo. That is Habidros in the hallway. He is Guesare's brother."

"Half-brother, my lady," murmured the minstrel. His eyes were fixed on the Lady Fachalana. So like his dead sister, yet so different. And he could feel that she was filled with the same power. For good or for evil?

That he could not tell, yet he sensed no malice.

Donzalo stepped forward and kissed the lady's hand. He, too, saw much alike to Jola in this woman but it did not affect him in the same way. She was not Jola and that was that.

This did not mean that she was not entangled somehow in his own destiny, and he in hers.

"My Lady Fachalana," he said, being as courtly as he knew how. For Donzalo, that mostly meant trying to avoid serious blunders.

She was tall, like Jola, perhaps even taller, and had much the same burnished skin tone. But her hair fell in dark waves where his lost love's had been golden and curling. Her eyes, too, were dark and as piercing as any he had ever seen.

"Sir Donzalo," she replied in turn. "It is good to meet you — at last."

Both knew the meaning behind that, the fleeting glimpses they had of each other in dream.

Guesare came out of his reverie and stepped forward as well to greet the young noblewoman. "My lady." He could feel the latent ability in her when he took her hand. The minstrel was almost afraid to touch his lips to it.

And Fachalana, too, sensed something in Guesare. Until now, her father was the only man of magic she had ever known.

"It is nearing the luncheon hour," said the ever-practical Blen. "Shall I order something from the kitchens?"

"An excellent idea, sir," replied Lady Lomela. "Traspa, will you take Ros to his nursery? I'll have something brought up for the two of you, as well."

The plump servant disappeared into the next room, sleepy boy in her arms.

Blen, his powers of observation as strong as ever, could feel something going on. There was a sense of anticlimax in the room. They had met — what now?

Lomela and Habidros — whom they finally prevailed upon to join them — seemed oblivious to it. But the other three — ah! Something was there but they were choosing to hide it behind good manners and small talk. They were still feeling each other out.

What will happen, he wondered, when Nafal and Maresta are thrown into this mix? Blen would just have to wait and see.

The men dispersed after lunch, leaving Lomela and her friend to further catch up, Blen lingering at the keep until time came for him to escort the Lady Fachalana back to their embassy. With the daughter of Lord Radal, best he do that in person.

~ ~ ~

"Madin."

Borrago's secretary looked up from the papers he was transcribing. "Sir Bolos?"

"I understand the count received visitors this morning." Bolos added nothing to this. Was it a question?

"Yes, my lord," said the scribe. If his master's son intended to be sparing with his words, then so would he.

And Bolos was not so obtuse that he did not recognize it. He took one of the chairs by his father's desk and sprawled in it.

"So, the Lady Fachalana — what is she like?"

Madin put down his stylus and smiled at the lordling. "Tall, sir," he answered.

Bolos chuckled at that. "So I have heard! And dark, too, if you had a mind to add it." He had always liked Madin, with his mix of dignity and dry humor. It let him get away with remarks that might not have been tolerated from others. "Did the meeting go well?"

"Such as it was, my lord, yes. Their time together was brief and I think neither wished to be there. The Lady Fachalana seemed eager to see your wife."

"Hmm, yes, they are longtime friends, the Lady Lomela has told me."

"I must say, sir, that Sir Blen appeared far the most interested individual there. He seems to enjoy watching people interact." Madin chuckled softly. "I also watch people at times, my lord."

"You have the perfect seat for that arena," observed Bolos.

"That I do, my lord, but your father expects discretion from me."

"And I would expect it no less," Bolos Rosam responded. A good man, he thought to himself, and not one I should seek to compromise. He is more valuable as who he is. He rose.

"A good evening to you, Madin."

"And to you, sir."

~ ~ ~

Fachalana thought much and said little about her day. Donzalo was not disappointing, but neither did he seem as exciting as she imagined. He did come off a bit bookish and awkward.

But how can anyone live up to ones dreams? She would have to get to know him better.

She wanted to know Guesare better, too. She was intrigued by the thought that he was a sorcerer, though apparently a rather minor one, a dabbler in magics. As she sat thinking, her friend entered from her adjoining apartment.

"These rooms are comfortable enough," said Ansa. They were. They were large and the windows allowed plenty of air on these warm nights. The appointments were far too masculine and functional, but that could be remedied.

"If only the building were not so ugly. It's hard to believe that Jobareth had a part in its design."

"We must blame Sir Blen as well. The two were thinking more of defense than of aesthetics." She spoke jokingly to her friend. "If only you could cast a spell to knock it down so they would be forced to start over."

"An excellent idea," said the Lady Fachalana, rising from her cushioned stool.

Fachalana decided to ham it up. She visualized herself as a wise and powerful sorcerer, wrapped in robes of sable, writ all over in mystic runes.

"I call upon the Demons of Droga!" she declaimed in her best and most serious stage tones. Fachalana had no idea who the demons were nor even whether Droga was a place or a person, but had seen the name in one of her father's books."Hear me, O Demons, and bring down this hideous house!"

Suddenly, the floor trembled below them.

Ansa's eyes grew wide and Fachalana cried out, 'No! No! Never mind!"

Then she grew silent, thinking on what had just happened. "So that's how it works," she whispered. She looked to her friend. "I need to *act* the spells. I need to put on the role of magician as I would any on the stage."

Fachalana spoke louder now, and with assurance. "This is how I can find the discipline I need. This is how I will have control. This is the key, Maresta!"

Ansa was not sure whether joy or fear was the proper response.

There came a rapping at the door. The Anian opened it to Mistress Murbalana. "My ladies," said she, "Sir Blen asked me to tell you that the ambassador just arrived, and your friend with him.

"Did you feel that earthquake? We never had such in Sharsh!" She shook her head. "The ground stays where it should, back home."

~ ~ ~

Gawis did not love his wife.

Indeed, he rarely thought of her at all. Their marriage had been a matter of politics, their daughters more the result of diplomacy than intimacy.

Yet he did not dislike Mara and felt it his duty to occasionally spend time with her and in her bed.

"Husband?" she said, after he had performed his duty and turned to sleep.

"What, Mara?" The princess rarely initiated a conversation with him. She was an exceedingly quiet and unassuming woman and Gawis did not mind that.

She pulled the covers close about her and sat up in bed. That was not modesty — child of the hot southern isles, Mara often felt chilled in her adopted land.

"Do you think my father tried to have Modareth murdered?"

"It is possible." The prince sat up as well, but let the bedclothes fall from his pale, compact frame. "Whoever is responsible, it bothers me greatly that they chose one from my circle to attempt the deed."

He had forgotten that Mara was one person to whom he might unburden himself. They talked so little anymore.

"Perhaps, Gawis," she began, hesitance obvious in her voice. "Perhaps it is a new circle that you need."

She could see his smile by the flicker of the candles, the smile that had charmed her when first they were wed. "That, my lady, I think is better advice than any other I have received lately."

He looked upon his wife, still a comely woman, and felt it might be a good idea to do his duty a second time this night.

## 11

"Our Lord Radal's daughter is upstairs?"

"She is, my lord," answered Sir Blen. "Would you wish to speak to her this night?"

"Oh, no, of course not. Even if she is not abed, I should be." Lord Doufan took a cursory look about the embassy's reception room and continued. "You can give me the tour tomorrow, sir. I suppose I should go present my credentials to the count, as well." He sighed with exaggerated weariness.

Jobareth Nafal smiled behind the ambassador's back. He had come to know the man well on their journey — as well as one might know such an enigma.

"Nafal, I shall see you in the morning. You, as well, Sir Blen. Now lead me to my rooms," Doufan said, turning to the majordomo. "And do have a bite sent up, too, won't you?

As the diplomat and his guide disappeared down a hallway — his apartment being here on the central floor — Jobareth took Blen aside. "Is Fachalana's companion with her?" he asked.

"She is. You know her true identity?"

"I do. I should have recognized her before from her stage appearances in Celatas." He barely whispered his next question. "Has Donzalo seen her?"

"No, not yet. It will be most interesting when he does, won't it?"

"That it will, Blen."

~ ~ ~

Blue and argent were the banners of Count Orgelo. It was a deeper blue than that on the Coradean arms, but clearly meant to honor that heritage. County Arvaram prided itself on the unbroken descent of its rulers from men of Lorj, men who had never surrendered to the Anians but had withdrawn their forces into the mountains and continued to fight.

It was Orgelo himself who came to Borrago's wedding, leaving his son Sorsen to rule in his stead. Sorsen was much loved throughout Lama, handsome, courtly and capable. He was also a bit of an ass, thought Orgelo, whose talents seemed better suited to battlefield and boudoir than to governing. But he loved his son.

On his way up the river, the count had heard rumors of roving bands terrorizing the countryside. Perhaps he should send his heir out to hunt them down once he returned to Tod-ford. It was the sort of thing Sorsen did well.

And his less powerful neighbors would not complain if his troops crossed their lands in pursuit. They expected Orgelo to keep the peace in their neighborhood.

Count Orgelo and his men had kept to the west of the Weldar all the way up to Ros-town, rather than crossing over to the Great Road. He felt more comfortable on what he considered his side of the river.

Now his men were boarding the ferry, under the watchful eye of Borrago's agent. The man seemed uncertain as to whether he should charge Orgelo for the crossing. He certainly did not intend to offer any payment, even if his entourage did require two trips across the Weldar.

This was, after all, an official visit.

Dawn. There was time to get his men encamped before he paid his respects to Borrago. The old dog, remarrying after all this time — it seemed politically dangerous. Couldn't he have just kept the woman his mistress?

Well, it would happen in ten days and what would come after, who knew?

~ ~ ~

Fachalana sat in the kitchens of the Sharshite embassy, thinking upon the previous evening and sipping hot barley-brew. Few were up and about this early, only a yawning scullery maid, a pair of grooms seeking their breakfast, a guardsman just off duty. They left her alone and that was what the Lady Fachalana wanted right then.

She realized that she had actually seen the Demons of Droga when she called upon them. She had entered, in part, into their realm.

It did not seem a place she would want to visit again. Had her

66

father been there? Maybe she should try contacting him again, with her new found ability.

Or not. It would not hurt to keep it a secret for a while.

"A good morning to you, my Lady Fachalana."

"Why, Lord Doufan. I would have expected you to sleep in, sir."

"May I sit?" When she nodded assent he took a chair across the table from her. It was quite a new table and still held the scent of pine. "I wished to explore this place before the official tour." Doufan kept his silence for a long moment.

"Nafal is a good man. Are you going to marry him, my lady?"

The noblewoman laughed aloud at the bold question. "I do not know, sir, I do not know."

"I would advise against it." This was even bolder. Who was Doufan to offer such advice?

"Explain, sir," she ordered.

"It is obvious that neither of you truly wishes to wed." He looked at her, and receiving no rebuttal, continued. "I could tell that from the way Jobareth spoke on our trip here and now I can see it in your eyes."

"What we wish may not matter in the long run," murmured Fachalana.

"My lady, it is all that matters. Have you seen the boy since our arrival?"

"No, my Lord Doufan. Shall I assume he will be with you at Keep Rosam most of the day?"

The ambassador considered the question briefly. "Perhaps I could leave him here and let Sir Blen escort me. I fear he would not like that, being very scrupulous in his duties. Moreover," he added, "Nafal does think he needs to keep an eye on me."

He laughed. "And perhaps he does."

~ ~ ~

Guesare had none of the power of his late sister, nor did he equal even his mother in magic. Still, he had felt the turmoil last night and knew it was the work of Fachalana.

He rode alone now, down to the embassy so that he might speak with the two young women. Little had been sorted out during yesterday's pleasantries; it was time for serious discussion.

Along the way, just before the road turned down toward the river, he passed a party of men, Nafal, Blen, a pair of guardsmen, and one he assumed to be the new ambassador. He only raised a hand in greeting and passed them by, not stopping to be introduced. This Lord Doufan seemed so nondescript that the minstrel would have been hard put to describe him a minute later.

Someone else was coming up the road now, a slight figure astride a galloping pony. It was the Anian girl herself. She reined her mount in as she reached the Cuddonian.

"Greetings, Mistress Ansa," said he.

"So, you have been speaking to my brother," she replied. "Please do not use that name again here."

"I will not," promised Guesare. "The secret of who you truly are is safe." He paused for only a second. "I think Donzalo has figured it out on his own."

He gave her a long look. "I do not believe I like the dark hair."

"My disguise?" Ansa laughed gaily and tossed her darkened locks. "And here I thought it would fool everyone!"

"It will not fool Donni. You do intend to see him, don't you?"

"Should I, Sir Guesare?" She turned her horse around. "Ride with me back to the embassy."

He clucked at his pony and moved forward to ride at the girl's side. "There would be no sense in hiding now," he said. No reply was forthcoming.

A minute later, he spoke again. "Were you with the Lady Fachalana last night?"

Ansa turned to him immediately. Her look told him all he needed.

"So you were," said Guesare. "What magic was she attempting?"

"It was only intended in play. The lady was as shocked as I when the earth shook."

"Ah." Guesare rode on a bit further before speaking again. "Fachalana is a danger. To Donzalo, to you, to herself."

"She means no harm. Of this I am certain. She — she has a crush on Donzalo."

The minstrel looked on her in astonishment. "So that is what this is all about?" Then he began to laugh. "Oh, I should have seen it!"

Guesare shook his head. "And Donni, ah, poor Donni, loved her sister." He had become of a sudden sober in his speech. "My sister."

He looked once more to Ansa, meeting her eyes. "Once, I think he may have loved you, too. Might you be the lady's rival?"

"I might," replied Ansa, "but I know not my course here."

She looks so like her brother, thought Guesare. Why did Donni see that and not I?

"The only proper course," said he, "is that which our heart sets us."

~ ~ ~

Blen had been up to Castle Rosam earlier, taking his morning exercise, and had confirmed that Borrago expected them. Sir Blen had become a surprisingly effective diplomat in Jobareth's absence.

It occurred to Jobareth, then, that Doufan and Blen were alike in many ways. He was not entirely willing to trust either.

"A luncheon, sir, is what the count suggested," Sir Blen was telling the ambassador, "preceded by a simple, family-only reception."

Lord Doufan nodded agreeably. He had made no discernible attempt to exercise his authority since arriving. The party was passing through the inner gate and into the courtyard before Borrago's hall.

Master of Arms Copago awaited them at its door. He and a pair of his men escorted the diplomats ceremoniously within.

There was Lomela. Jobareth could not go over and greet her right now, as he might have wished, as he might have done on most occasions. She stood at her husband's side as Doufan was introduced.

That he was charming her, as he did most, was obvious. And Bolos too.

Gruff Borrago, he suspected, would be more immune. An aide came to that man's side and whispered something in his ear. The count nodded in assent.

"Lord Orgelo has just arrived," he announced aloud. "He will join us shortly."

Nafal could not help notice the look of displeasure that crossed Bolos's face. Perhaps no one in the room missed it.

After a couple minutes, Count Borrago and the ambassador went aside to speak privately and the guests mingled more casually.

There was Donzalo, making his way toward him. And who was that large fellow who seemed his shadow? "*Legate* Nafal!" He exclaimed, emphasizing his new title. Jobareth was surprised that Donzalo embraced him. That was new.

"This is my kinsman and bodyguard Habidros," said the Laman, gesturing toward his tall companion. "He's Guesare's brother."

The two bowed wordlessly to each other. "Father insists that he accompany me everywhere. Not that either of us minds.

"So, Jobareth, how fare you these days?"

This was neither the time nor place to unburden himself to his young friend. "Well, enough, *Sir* Donzalo," he replied, echoing the emphasis on newly acquired title. "And glad to have fared back to my friends here at last." Does that sound hollow? he wondered. Have I become too much the diplomat?

He did not realize Donzalo was directing their way to Lady Lomela until they were almost before her.

"My lady," he said, and took her hand.

"At last! You certainly took your time, Jobareth Nafal." The Princess Lomela laughed with true pleasure. "Welcome back, my friend."

"Lunch," whispered Habidros in Donzalo's ear.

"Oh, we're being served," said the young Laman. "And there's Count Orgelo, arrived just in time for a free meal!" Lady Lomela's husband was already at the table and lost in his own thoughts, so Donzalo took her one arm and Jobareth, the other, and escorted her.

STEPHEN BROOKE

For a few moments, it seemed like the way things once were.

## 12

Guesare had parted from Ansa at the bottom of the embassy hill. Some other day, perhaps, he could meet with Radal's daughter. He had a better idea of motives, now, of Fachalana's, of Ansa's. Indeed, of his own.

Play-acting, eh? If the Sharshite noblewoman caused that much ruckus without intending, what could happen if she truly harnessed her abilities? She might not be the equal of Jola but she was not that far less.

The woman's whole life is acting, isn't it? he asked himself. She has cast herself as Donzalo's lover, his destiny. Might she actually be intended for that role?

Ansa seemed a practical person. She would not pursue Donzalo thoughtlessly, hopelessly. Maybe she needs to, thought Guesare. Maybe she needs to be less the spy, less like her scheming brother, and find her happiness.

Of course, there was also always the possibility that Radal was somehow using his daughter to get at Donzalo. It should never be forgotten that the sorcerer still wanted him dead.

Ahead of him lay Borrago's castle and many choices.

~ ~ ~

It was more than a week until the Summer Fair had its official start, yet tents and booths were already sprouting on Borrago's wide fairground.

"We'll need to secure a good spot," said Galaro's second. "It's none too soon."

"You pick a likely place or two and I'll go find the marshal to pay our fees. If Borrago has raised them again, I'll curse him even more loudly than the last time!"

"Aren't those some of Orgelo's men?" said the trader, peering at a group with his good eye.

"He or his son must have come for the wedding. That should bring in even larger crowds than usual. Ha, old Borrago should marry anew every year!"

He set off in search of the harried fellow who organized this fair with the help of far too few assistants. It was fortunate that the many merchants here did a good job of policing themselves through the month-long event.

The afternoon sun beat upon the tall Cuddonian. He could feel the perspiration dripping down his beard.

"Ho, Galaro!" one of the other merchants greeted him. "Which direction are you smuggling goods this season?"

"South to north," roared the trader in response, "but I'm about to switch it around!"

He continued across the grounds, skirting groups of men intent on erecting multi-hued pavilions, greeting rivals who were, for the most part, also friends. There stood a couple of the Rosam soldiers in their colors of green and sable. "Tell me, my bullies, be the marshal about?"

One pointed toward a small hill rising by the field, and a grayish tent upon it. "He's set up shop up there," said the fellow. "Says it's easier to keep an eye on all of you."

"An excellent idea. I thank you, sirs." And a good way to avoid our complaining, thought Galaro, if we have to go all the way over there and climb a hill each time.

When he finally reached the man, he found that the fees had, indeed, increased again. And he did curse Borrago most roundly.

~ ~ ~

"It is good, my lady, to have young Master Jobareth back."

Traspa had never gotten used to referring to Nafal as Lector. Would she ever learn to call him Legate?

"Yes, Traspa. It is too bad his duties kept him from remaining this afternoon. How I would love to sit and talk as once we did!"

"That ambassador can't keep him busy all the time, my lady. I'm sure we'll see more of the boy. Here, don't eat that!" The maid removed a bit of ribbon from young Ros's mouth. "Your mother needs it for her new dress."

The child took Mistress Traspa's admonition without complaint.

He was a notably good-natured boy, albeit active and apt to get himself into places he should not be.

Lady Lomela found herself wandering out onto her little balcony. The sun shone fully upon it at this time of day. There was Guesare riding in. Where had he been?

She would not mind sitting and talking with the minstrel too. The princess remembered how he had pleased the late Lady Vibola with his songs and his tales, full of both adventure and amusement.

Yes, she must have Guesare and Donzalo visit, and Jobareth, when he could. Donzalo could even bring his bodyguard cousin along. The man could be interesting when he chose to speak, full of stories of his life as a mercenary.

Why not bring back all that Lady Vibola had, when she was the grand dame of this household? That role had fallen to Lomela now. Sima would never be a rival to her, nor seek to be, even when she became a countess next week.

Lady Lomela turned back into her sitting chamber, carefully closing the doors behind her. A breeze would have been welcome on this warm afternoon but little Ros could not be trusted. He would be out there as soon as their backs were turned. One could wager on that.

There was little else the lady was willing to wager on right then.

~ ~ ~

Pol had settled into the barracks of the new embassy, a spacious room on the basement level. His companion on their recent journey, the young diplomat Benawis, now resided in a small room two floors above him, ready at hand for his duties as secretary to the legate.

He knew Nafal did not want to show him any particular attention now they were back in County Rosam. Pol would be a more effective spy for his master that way.

Maybe he could show Benawis around Ros-town once things settled down a bit here. Something about the fellow gnawed at Pol. He had seemed too ready to befriend the young soldier. Pol, for his part, had been willing to act the naïve country boy when he was with him.

As he had been willing to act his friend. Pol was not sure he actually liked the secretary very much.

Night guard duty. He'd better grab a bite and get to his post.

~ ~ ~

"You may leave us, Lector"

Benawis bowed to his master and, with a perhaps slightly-too-long look at the two rather attractive young women in the room, exited.

None of the three had missed it. "My secretary appreciates feminine beauty," said Jobareth. "Or maybe just anything feminine."

Ansa laughed. Fachalana did not. "I dislike him," she stated.

Then she seemed to remember something. "The man visited Father," she said, "before you left with the ambassador." The noblewoman sniffed. "I did not like him then, either."

"Probably when he was being considered for this post," Jobareth surmised. But it was unusual for the great Lord Radal to be interviewing so minor a diplomat.

"Anyway, I hear that you visited the town this afternoon, while I was busy with my duties."

"I gave Lady Fachalana the complete tour," said Ansa, "ending up at the fairgrounds. They are only starting to fill up but it will a marvel when they do."

"We must visit again next week," Fachalana stated. "I should have brought more money with me!"

"And who would cart everything back to Sharsh?" asked her companion.

Jobareth smiled. "I can't help with cartage but this may prove a boon to your finances." He handed a dispatch to Fachalana.

Ansa brought her head in close so she could read it too. Wonder crept across her visage.

"A viscountess, Lana?"

"And a position at court. There will be an income attached to that. Maybe to the title as well." Jobareth chuckled. "Maybe I *should* marry you. For your money, you know."

"With your grandfather one of the wealthiest men in Sharsh?" replied Fachalana. " A thought came to her. "Why, I will officially have a higher title than my father." Lord Radal had always refused high rank, feeling he could work most effectively with no title other than lord.

King Lareth had reluctantly agreed, knowing that elevating his friend might cause ill feeling among the old nobility. Or perhaps, considering Radal's reputation, ill feeling among pretty much everyone.

"This will be interesting," continued the lady. "It doesn't have much bearing on what we do here in Lama though. I'll worry about it when we get home." Assuming I ever go home, she told herself. If her destiny were truly entwined with that of Donzalo, might she not remain here?

Suddenly, she laughed. "What will Lomela think of this? We must go visit her tomorrow, the three of us. Do find time for it, Jobo."

"I will, my ladies. I consider it another of my diplomatic duties."

~ ~ ~

"You see, my dear, we arrived in plenty of time."

Lady Thara nodded absentmindedly. "I should seek out Sima and see if she needs any help."

"She has Sir Copago's wife and the Lady Lomela and probably every other woman in the keep to assist her. Relax, wife of mine. Let's get to our rooms.

"Assuming my brother hasn't given them away to some other of his guests."

That brother had watched from his tower window as the little caravan entered the courtyard. He could talk to Paren in the morning. Let his stewards attend to him and Thara tonight.

He looked at the stack of documents on his desk and his secretary, Madin, waiting patiently, and the count sighed. Borrago would not be visiting his bride-to-be this night. So much to be done.

Would that Bolos could take some of this load. But he did not trust his heir's judgment nor did he care for his secretive ways since he had become a sober man. Maybe after the wedding he should send him out to visit their many allies scattered through Lama. That would give the boy something useful to do.

He took one more glimpse from the window and turned to his work.

## 13

No one had taken any notice of Ansa as they entered the castle. Why would they connect her with a serving girl who had spent a few weeks in Keep Rosam, nearly a year ago?

Lomela thought her familiar and then thought no more on it.

It was Mistress Traspa who knew her the moment she laid eyes on the girl. "Why, Posena! What has happened to your hair?"

And then immediately asked, "Does Master Donzalo know you are here?"

"Posena?" repeated the Lady Lomela, turning her gaze to the Anian. "Oh!"

"We know her as Maresta," said Fachalana. "She is my friend." She had to follow this by again telling the tale of Ansa's mission to Lama and her role in instigating it, with more detail than she had ever provided Jobareth.

Satisfied with the explanation, Traspa went to attend to her duties elsewhere. She had taken charge of young Ros, as she had of the boy's mother, and took the responsibility most seriously. But she still wondered if Donzalo knew that girl was here.

They spoke of many things, those four, through the morning and most of it was of little import. Eventually, the talk did turn to the young Laman knight.

"The ladies have explained to me why your father yearns for Donzalo's death," said Nafal. "Shall I tell it?" he asked them. The two women nodded an assent.

"The gist of it, Lomela, is that the king fears he poses a threat to Ros and his inheritance. The Oracle at Cars handed down a prophecy that the son of Donzalo will rule in Lama."

Lomela seemed very much taken aback at this news. None of the three had expected it to shake her so.

"His son?" she whispered. "His son." Then a half-smile played on her lips. "You have often seen his son here, Jobareth. He has played in your lap, Lana."

It was their turn to be astounded.

Suddenly, the princess was on her feet. "I must write my father and tell him this!"

"No," spoke Ansa. "A letter might be intercepted. What if your husband learned of it?" She has her wits about her, thought Jobareth. And knows her spy-craft as well, I would wager.

"Maresta is right," he said. "It would be far too dangerous. Such news would need be delivered to the king in person."

"I could tell him when we return," said Fachalana, reluctantly. She did not want to go back to Sharsh anytime soon and maybe not ever.

"What of your father?" asked Lady Lomela. "Could we tell him of this?"

"I do not think the prophecy drives him anymore. He has other reasons to hate Donzalo." Fachalana did not intend to speak of those things she had learned of her sister and of her death. "He might use this as a weapon.

"Why not come back to Sharsh with us for a visit?" she asked, with sudden inspiration. "You could tell your father yourself."

~ ~ ~

"He was sitting by the road, sir, as bold as can be."

"And you are sure it was this Perdos?" asked Captain Corgos.

"Aye, sir, though he looked like he'd been through some rough living and his beard lay on his chest."

I'll send out a patrol to check this, thought Sir Corgos. Best to be safe.

"All he wanted, as I said, sir, was the latest news from down at Keep Rosam." The man, a peddler who visited from time to time, continued. "And he did ask if there was a minstrel there. What with him being banished and all, I thought you should know."

"It is well done and I thank you. I know the ladies of the keep will want to see your wares and hear your gossip, so I'll leave you to them."

Still after that Guesare, is he? I can't fault him for that but I can't permit him to loiter on the roads either. Not on my watch.

~ ~ ~

There he stood, even taller than Ansa remembered, and no longer looking a boy.

"Donzalo," she whispered.

He strode across the room, paying no mind to the other three and spoke. "I ask again as I did when last I saw you: who are you, truly?"

She found herself uncertain as to her reply.

"Her name is Ansa," said the man standing in the doorway. "I am sorry, Ansa, but he should know the truth." Guesare turned his eyes toward the Lady Fachalana. "As should you, my lady."

"Oh, you mean that my friend is an Anian spy," Fachalana cooly replied. "I had figured that one out, though it did take me a while." She looked at the young woman seated beside her. "Ansa, is it? I like the name."

Donzalo turned to the minstrel. "She is related to Oder, isn't she?"

"He is my brother," said the girl.

Jobareth Nafal and the Princess Lomela were understandably confused by this exchange.

"You are Ani?" asked the diplomat.

Ansa nodded. "Born and raised on the high steppes, Legate."

"But she spoke truly when she said Lady Fachalana sent her here before," said Guesare. "Not that it might not have fitted well into some Anian scheme or another."

Donzalo stood in silence and pondered all of this. A few moments earlier he had been the least well informed person in this room.

Fachalana noticed his hand go to the silver brooch he wore ever at his shoulder, a brooch in the likeness of a wolf. Hadn't she glimpsed something like it in the dream world where she first saw Donzalo? It had been so brief, she was not sure now.

But she did sense that there was some sort of power in it. She had not recognized that two days ago.

"Then, Ansa," said the Laman knight, "since we have now been properly introduced, may I welcome you to Castle Rosam?"

80

~ ~ ~

"He's a man of habit," said the cloaked figure. "He comes down that pathway, if he comes at all, and he comes always by foot." He pointed out the route on the scrap of paper he held.

Sojel nodded. Was there more?

"And his dog is always with him."

Dogs could cause problems. "How about in the morning?"

"Back the same way. But his son sometimes walks with him."

The sergeant folded the crude map and stuck it in his belt. "Good enough. Our master will be pleased with your work." That was high praise from Sojel and, perhaps, unlike him. But he liked the fact that things were moving again and seemingly in the correct direction.

Both men disappeared into the dusk.

~ ~ ~

"You should not have come, Uncle, if you did not want to be put to work."

"It always seems to fall on you and me, boy, doesn't it?"

"Someone has to show them how things are properly done," replied Donzalo. He and Sir Paren had spent most of the day on the logistics of the upcoming wedding. It was a welcome break to the young man from the drama of the previous days. It was an opportunity to think on things while busying his hands.

They had worked late into the evening. It was only six days now — well, it would be, come morning — till the event and much was to be done.

"So we shall have the procession begin — here," said Paren, pushing a stake into the ground, "and then out the main gate."

"I still think it would be easier if we formed up outside the keep," opined Donzalo.

"We would never get them together out there. The more impatient would take off down the road before we got everyone else in line.

"At any rate, I think we are done for this day," Sir Paren said. "Let's get back to the hall and see if they held some supper for us."

81

# THE SIGN OF THE ARROW

"My lords! My lords!" A soldier was running toward them over the green.

"What is it man?" called Donzalo, holding his lantern high.

"The count has been slain!"

# OF EXILES: THE SEVENTH TALE

## 1

"It was the dog, sir. We heard him howling."

King strained at the end of a rope. "He didn't want to leave his master," claimed the soldier at the other end.

"Was there any sign of who was responsible?" asked Bolos, now Count Bolos. "Any sign at all?"

Another man at arms held out a bit of blue cloth. "We think the dog may have torn it from the assassin."

It was the blue of the Arvaram. Everyone there could see that.

Sir Copago thought finding the scrap overly convenient but held his tongue.

To his surprise, his half-brother did not. "It might be planted," said Bolos. "We will make no conclusions now."

The new count could see no reason why Orgelo would want to kill his father. All Borrago's recent actions had been favorable to their relationship.

He looked at Copago. The same could be said of that man. The marriage of Borrago and his mother could only help him.

Indeed, the man who stood most to gain was Bolos himself. That upset him. He was weary of intrigue and politics and all the worries that had surrounded him lately. He was weary of losing those he loved.

Could his father-in-law have a part in this? Could Bolos have brought it on with his own letters to the king?

"Bring the body to the hall," he ordered. Sir Copago motioned for the men to bear it forward. What was to be done with Sir Copago?

By Kamat! swore Bolos to himself. I opposed this wedding but I would not have had it become a funeral.

~ ~ ~

"With County Rosam in turmoil, I must urge you to leave for home as soon as possible."

Lord Doufan sat behind the largest desk Ansa had ever seen, flanked by Jobareth Nafal and Sir Blen. The ambassador's secretary sat inconspicuously in a corner.

"Have I time to say goodbye to Lady Lomela?" asked Fachalana, in a quite even, matter-of-fact voice. She's in role, thought Ansa. It really does help her control her emotions.

Nafal spoke. "I shall convey any messages for you, my ladies. Our Lord Doufan is right — you should be on the road immediately."

The ambassador nodded. "I will not order this," he said, "but I think it would be wise for Sir Blen to accompany you." This was news to Blen.

Doufan turned to him. "I can not think of anyone better qualified, sir, nor whom I would more trust with this mission. Moreover, I wish you to go straight to the king with my report on this situation."

Of course, a courier was already speeding westward with the news.

"Very well, sir," replied the knight. The request made sense to him and Blen was a very sensible man. He addressed the two women. "We will travel faster without your servants. They can follow later with one of the guardsmen. I and the other will ride with you."

"Best cross in a boat or two, rather than the ferry," said Jobareth. "Bolos may have closed cross-river traffic." Blen nodded agreement.

Ansa rose. "We can be ready in an hour," she said.

They were across the Weldar in two.

~ ~ ~

There came a knock on their cottage door, an almost timid knock. Janona opened it to the Lady Lomela, accompanied only by her ever-faithful maid, Traspa.

Lomela crossed the room at once to where Dame Sima sat with her son, the acolyte Grippo, and embraced the woman. They sat a while in silent, tearless grief.

Traspa, waiting by the door, could not hold her own tears. Janona gently escorted her to a seat at the table, where she sobbed quietly. The wife of Sir Copago then busied herself with the making of tea. One custom the Ani had left behind was the drinking of tea. Most Lamans did not know of its connection to the hated invaders of their land.

Those who did, ignored it.

They spoke for a time, Lomela and Sima, and their speech was inconsequential, full of remembrance and regret and condolence. Then the princess asked a question that was, indeed, of consequence.

"What now, Sima? Will you remain here?"

"Your husband may not permit that, my lady," came from Grippo, who had remained silent until that moment.

"He would not force you to leave! I would not permit it."

"No, my lady," said Sima, "he would not throw us out but he will most certainly discharge Copago from his service. How could we remain here, then?" She let her vision wander about the little cottage, so long her home. "All things end, don't they, Grippo?"

"Please don't ask me for sermons, Mother." He remained quiet for a moment, before saying, all in a rush, "I will not take my vows this year. My family is more important."

"No," objected Sima, "your brother can take care of us. You have worked long to become a priest."

"There may be little prospect for him as priest now in County Rosam," said Janona, bringing tea to the table. She poured out a cup for Traspa, who, being a good Sharshite, would have preferred wine. "Would you care for some, my lady?" she asked Lomela.

"Yes, thank you." The Lady Lomela turned back to mother and son. "Janona is right. Grippo's fortunes will ever be tied to those of his brother." She sipped politely from the cup handed her before setting it aside. "Waiting a year might be wise and, after all," added Lomela with a smile, "this family may need Grippo more right now than Kamat does."

The three Lamans nodded at that. They understood duty.

My mistress knows her Lamans, doesn't she? thought Traspa, who then spoke aloud. "My lady, we'd best get back."

"Yes, Traspa, we should." Lomela rose. "I suspect my husband will have much need of me in the days that come."

~ ~ ~

Jobareth Nafal was not pleased by the absence of his master of arms. Yes, it was important that Blen accompany the women back to Sharsh but the defense of the embassy was important as well. The other fighting men here were ordinary soldiers, not leaders nor tacticians.

"I do not expect trouble from the Lamans, my lord," he told the ambassador, once the travelers were on their road home, "but I would want to be prepared for the eventuality."

"They may suspect that Sharsh has a hand in this," stated Lord Doufan, and added, quite matter-of-factly, "I suspect it myself."

"The king would order this?" asked the younger man.

The ambassador sighed. "He is certainly capable of it." He considered that statement for a moment and then continued. "His councilor Radal would be more likely to order such an action. He has become used to having his way and acting independently.

"And he wants Donzalo," Doufan added, looking up to meet Nafal's eyes. "You know that."

"You know of the — prophecy, sir?"

"Lareth himself filled me in before we left Celatas. And who, sir," asked the ambassador, with arched brow, "filled you in?"

Jobareth smiled wanly. "The Lady Fachalana, my lord. She has been know to, ah, peruse her father's papers."

"I can believe it," said Lord Doufan. "I can very much believe it."

~ ~ ~

"How fares your mother?"

"She — copes, my lord."

"Please convey my condolences to her, Sir Copago. I extend them to you as well." Count Orgelo thought of his own wife of some thirty years, back in Tod-ford, and wondered, fleetingly, whether he could bear her loss. How much harder would it be to have happiness torn away from one, just as it was finally being given?

"I thank you, my lord," replied Copago, eying the men milling around them. "I should to my duties."

"You know, my boy, that those duties may soon be taken from you. Bolos has never loved you.

"Know, too, that there is always a place for you in my service. My son likes you, even if you have unhorsed him from time to time." Orgelo rubbed at his unshaven jaw. Though the count's long hair remained as black as in his youth, Copago could see that the whiskers were peppered with gray. "It would be good for him to have someone like you at his side."

"It seems soon to be considering it, my lord, but I thank you for the offer. For now, I remain the man of the Count Rosam, whoever that may be."

Orgelo nodded gravely as the knight returned to his post. A good man, yes, and the fact that he could just possibly claim his father's inheritance didn't hurt any.

~ ~ ~

It had become obvious that Sir Blen — and probably Jobareth too — had an emergency plan in place for just such an occasion. Blen had led them swiftly down less traveled roads to a house by the river. It was a shabby, slouching, low-built house near where the Abam joined the Weldar and the men there asked no questions. They were taken across in a barge with muffled oars.

The party traveled through the night and most of the next day before stopping at an inn. "We are in Count Dordos's lands now," the knight told them, "beyond any harm that might come from County Rosam."

Dordos was thoroughly dependent on his Sharshite paymasters and would not think of crossing them.

That evening, Fachalana attempted the link with her father. It came easier than ever before.

*Fachalana.*

She could sense his pleasure in this demonstration of her ability.

*Count Borrago has been murdered,* she told him.

Her father said nothing.

He knows this already, she thought. Is he behind it?

*You are returning home?* he asked.

*Yes, Father. It seemed best.*

Radal did not comment on that. *You have grown,* he said.

*I am learning, Father.*

*That you are. We must talk on it when you reach here.*

He seemed distracted by something or someone with him in his tower room.

*Farewell,* said Lord Radal and unilaterally broke their connection.

Well, certainly her father was a busy man. Walking into his mind was little different than walking into his office — he couldn't be expected to drop everything to talk to her!

Ansa was sitting on her bed in the room they shared, staring at her. "Where were you?" she asked.

"At Mountain Keep," answered Fachalana truthfully. She felt very tired, both from their journey and the strain of forming the link. I hope it gets easier with practice, she thought.

"And now I have returned and the only place I wish to be is asleep."

## 2

Radal had not known that Count Borrago was dead. This is not to say he did not expect the event.

Now he would expect a messenger, hastily bringing the news. Two, in fact, one from his own agent and one from the embassy. He turned back to the magic with which he had been occupied, here in his high tower, when Fachalana had made contact.

She had grown stronger. No, the girl had always been strong — she was learning to control her strength. Allowing her to travel, to be beyond his influence for a while, had brought unexpected rewards.

He did wish she had remained in County Rosam. Radal might still have been able to use her in some way to further his plans there.

A little sprite-like being spoke to him. It was not in the room nor was he with it, truly, but each had entered in some part into another world. When he did not wish to be troubled with forming a link such creatures as these were the best and least tiring way to send messages swiftly and secretly. The spirits of the winds would go by ways only known to them and speak the words with which they were charged.

Radal had many such messages to send. Things were moving now and he was the one who had provided the impetus, for better or worse. It had to be done, no matter what Lareth had ordered.

He smiled mirthlessly at his attempt to rationalize his own actions to himself. Mankind is but a flicker in the great darkness, he told himself. None of it matters.

Nothing but vengeance for the life of one daughter, the daughter he had not known, and the realization of the other's gifts.

~ ~ ~

"You do not blame Count Orgelo for this?"

Bolos looked at his uncle for a moment, as if not understanding the question. Then he spoke and his words were bitter.

"I blame Orgelo and I blame Copago and I blame even his mother. I blame the king in Sharsh and I blame his dog Radal. Most of all, I blame you, Donzalo. All the turmoil of this past year has been centered on you."

Sir Paren's eyes turned to the third man in the room, Donzalo Rosam.

"I would serve you how I can, Brother," was the only reply from the young knight.

"As I did your father," Paren reminded his nephew. "It is good to have someone to depend on."

"Stay or go. I do not care." Bolos turned to survey the courtyard from the narrow window. This was his office now, here in the tower where Borrago had so long resided.

"Why not come home with me, Donni? Aid me in the running of the estate," said Paren.

Bolos's words came cold. "I have not yet named him your heir."

Then he sighed and turned back to his family. "Ah, forgive me. You are welcome here, Donzalo, and I will continue the allowance our father set upon you." He shook his head. "But trouble follows you. It might serve both of us better were you elsewhere.

"I do have one great favor to ask of you, Uncle. Give me Sir Corgos as my new master of arms. No, I can not have Copago here any longer. I know he served my father well and I know that he is family. But I must and will have my own man.

"Jak would never do. He is loyal but not suited to the task."

"I will ask him on our return. He may not wish to leave the comfortable life he has found at my keep." I most certainly would not, added Sir Paren to himself.

~ ~ ~

"The count has discharged my brother, as expected. He will serve only until Summer Feast."

"Being who he is, he will serve faithfully to the last moment, eh?" asked Jobareth.

"Most certainly," replied Brother Grippo, "but Bolos has also set a somewhat generous sum of money on him to ease the departure. And perhaps to ease the count's conscience as well.

"He does not hate Copago, I think. He simply wants him gone."

Jobareth Nafal agreed with his assessment. The man was level-headed and a reliable source of information. Maybe he should be on his informal payroll.

"You still intend to forgo your ordination?" he asked.

Grippo only nodded.

Jobareth questioned further. "Where then?"

"Sir Paren has offered a place for our family at his keep. I will accompany them there and, perhaps, remain. Along with," he chuckled, "Donzalo's books."

"I heard that he was moving them all again. To his uncle's?"

"He thought it the safest place to store them. I do not think he intends to remain at Castle Rosam."

Nafal leaned forward to refill Grippo's goblet from a frosted pitcher. Chilled wine seemed unknown here in Lama and he had missed it, especially on hot nights such as these. Fortunately, there was a spring-house not far from this new town dwelling and they were quite willing to keep a cask or two cool for him.

From the high porch — it seemed every decent house in Ros-town had a high porch — he could see mist rising from the river. Beyond it, Sir Blen and the women must be well on their way home.

He would have to let Blen know he approved of this house he had taken for them.

"Your brother won't go to Sir Paren's keep, will he?"

"No, Legate. He has said not yea nor nay but he is giving serious thought to joining Count Orgelo's service."

~ ~ ~

Some mourners were gathered in the hall. Others stood outside the great doors, flung open to the clear morning air.

Borrago lay on his bier, his body wrapped in green silk. Beneath the silk, nothing, as it was believed that one should return to Kamat as one came. This was not so much a Kamatian belief as a Laman one, and in keeping with their tendency toward austerity.

The hierophant intoned a passage, known well to most of those in attendance.

# THE SIGN OF THE ARROW

*As an arrow flies my soul,*
*into darkness, into night;*
*none whom I have left behind*
*sees the ending of its flight.*

The mourners responded.

*Flies to Kamat, ever watchful,*
*waiting in the realm of light.*

Two acolytes raised censers above the late count's bier. Fragrant smoke floated toward the ceiling beams and the high priest continued.

*As a comet through the sky,*
*burning with creation's flame;*
*as an arrow flies my soul,*
*without substance, without name.*

*Flies to Kamat, ever waiting,*
*to the one from whence we came.*

The crowd murmured their answering prayer and began to fall into a column behind the cart bearing Count Borrago's mortal remains, passing in slow procession from the hall, through the courtyard and toward the gates of Castle Rosam.

~ ~ ~

"If we keep to this pace, we can reach Mountain Keep by the solstice," Sir Blen told his charges. "We are better than half-way there now."

"He seeks to train us as couriers," Ansa confided — albeit in a rather loud voice — to her companion.

"You, my lady," responded the knight, "need no training, I think."

Are these two flirting? wondered Lady Fachalana. She was too weary to give it much thought. Didn't her father have drugs that helped him carry on? She should ask him when they reach the keep.

Now that she had learned how to look into all the many worlds other than our own, she was having trouble keeping them out. Things and places and voices filled her dreams, when Fachalana was able to sleep at all.

Did Blen know that Ansa was Anian? She couldn't remember for sure — oh, right, only Jobareth and his circle at the Keep Rosam were in on it. Donzalo knew.

Donzalo. When would she see him again? *Would* she see him again? Her chance to know him had been torn from her as soon as she had reached for it. With the turmoil she and Ansa had left behind them, it seemed unlikely that they could again soon travel to Lama.

"I fear we may need to tie the lady in her saddle," Ansa whispered to Blen, as they rode on toward the marches of Sharsh.

## 3

The procession wound from the castle gates, following the markers Donzalo and Paren had set out for a very different ceremony, only three days earlier. The column turned not right, as most did, not toward the town nor toward the stoa where many of their Kamatian rites were held. Left they went, on a less-traveled, narrower road that gradually grew steeper.

Near the gates, it passed the cottage of Copago, that road, and then other cots until the ground grew too rocky for farmer or even shepherd. Below a craggy outcropping, jutting into the sky like an arrow aimed toward the heavens, they paused.

Paren motioned toward the two carts loaded with the required wood. Men came forward and began carrying the bundled staves up stairs roughly carved into the rock. Pine and oak was the wood; they would know how to lay it properly.

Bolos, Donzalo, Paren and Galaro each took a corner to bear the bier up to the high place — it had been realized that Galaro, if one did not acknowledge Copago, was the next closest relative to the late count in attendance. Bolos, of course, was not willing to acknowledge Copago.

But he did not forbid his attendance. Count Bolos had no ill will toward his half-brother. He wanted only to have nothing more to do with him and all the things of which he was a reminder.

He did, however, forbid the presence of the Sharshite diplomats at this ceremony, even his wife's friend Jobareth. The ambassador had been allowed to attend the funeral but Bolos would not have him here. Bolos wished he could have banned Count Orgelo, as well, but that would have been an unnecessary insult.

Bolos also wished briefly that his three fellow pallbearers were not all a head taller than he.

The pyre was ready by the time they finished their ascent. It was fitting that a man return to Kamat this way, by flame, here on a high place where his ashes might be scattered by the winds.

Carefully they placed the pallet atop the pile and stepped aside for the hierophant. That man was lighting his torch from the brazier they had carried along — getting a fire going could be a tricky job in these high windy spots. Then the high priest approached and wordlessly set the wood, now well soaked with oil, aflame.

He stepped back and made the sign of arrow, as did the rest of the mourners, both those on the crag and those waiting below, and turned to begin his descent.

~ ~ ~

"Come with me," ordered Sir Copago.

Donazalo had been occupied with the packing up of his varied belongings, but he followed the man without question. Copago had such an effect.

"Have you chosen new quarters?" asked the master of arms as Donzalo followed him down the hall.

"I thought I might take my old ones back."

"I have a better idea," said Copago and then said no more, leading onward.

The way led them past Donzalo's former rooms and then down a flight of stairs to the ground level. Only barracks and stables occupied this area, Donzalo knew. He also knew that the room before which they now stood was used for nothing but to store tack. Copago drew forth a ponderous key to open the heavy, iron-banded door.

"These were, long ago, the quarters of the Anian commanders when they held this keep," said the knight. "Before any of the rest of it was built." He carefully barred the door behind them.

"Your father —"

"Our father," interrupted Donzalo.

"Yes, our father, showed me a secret here. It is unknown to Bolos or anyone else alive. Now I will show it to you."

The room was somewhat narrow, though long. Donzalo suspected that it might once have been divided in two, as were his old quarters a floor above. Directly above? Possibly. Close, anyway. As in his former rooms, the far end was the castle wall itself, though at this level the stacked stone merged with the solid rock below it.

Copago was near that wall, busying himself with the moving of some of the detritus that had accumulated in this room. Much of it was overflow from the stables, old saddles, faded blankets, empty containers someone thought might be useful someday. He motioned the younger man over.

"Here," he said, and showed him a hidden latch. A panel opened, a narrow doorway to darkness. Donzalo held his lantern before him and looked within to spy a steep staircase, practically a ladder, cut into the stone that lay beneath Keep Rosam.

Copago chuckled. "I think you will fit, boy. Go on down."

Seeing he would need both hands free to negotiate his way, Donzalo grasped the bail of his lantern in his teeth and started down. Thankfully, the stairway was short and he was soon standing on a more or less level floor.

"It is easy going from here," said his guide, squeezing by him. They followed a cramped passageway — low enough that Donzalo could not stand upright — that slowly sloped downward, here and there broken by a stair or two. Within a minute, he could see light coming from ahead.

"I think this cave is natural," said Sir Copago, as they entered a larger space, "and the Anians carved out our passageway to it. Also," he added, with a nod toward a large rock around which sunlight filtered into the chamber, "they hid its entrance."

There was a narrow way, to the right and hidden from eyes below, where one might slip between the rock and the cliff face and step out onto a ledge. It was a very narrow ledge and Donzalo did not like standing there.

Copago pointed. "There is a way down here. See? Just follow the ledge. I have little doubt the Anians cut it into the cliff wall. It will carry you over to that spur and beyond it lies a wooded slope that is easy to negotiate.

"We wouldn't attempt that in daylight and risk being seen. I went down it once at night. And then back up, of course. If fact, we'd better get back inside now and take no chances."

Donzalo took a second to peer upward. The castle walls could not be seen from here. So they could not be seen from the castle walls.

"You may show this to my replacement, if you feel it wise. But," warned Copago, "I would tell no others."

~ ~ ~

"Are you bored, Brother?"

"That I am, Galaro," responded the minstrel Guesare. "This place has little to offer when its people are in mourning."

"They will throw off their somber garments and come pouring into the fair in two days. But that is not the real reason, is it? Being banned from Keep Rosam and your noble friends there is the root of this mood of yours.

"I know, too," added Galaro, "that you like to know what is going on. Why," he said with a wink, "one might think you a professional spy!"

"Please, Brother, say that not in public."

The big Cuddonian laughed outright. "This fairground is fairly riddled with spies. I am sure at least two in my company report to someone. Not my competitors, I hope."

"Nobos is in the employ of Count Orgelo," asserted Guesare. "I know him of old." He put his rebec aside and took up the flagon of ale by his side, first checking for flies afloat in the brew.

Galaro took a seat beside him in the shade of the tent fly. "Nobos, eh? Well, no harm in that. Old Orgelo is just keeping an eye on his investments."

"I may ride south with the count after Summer Feast," said Guesare quietly. "I and Sir Copago."

"Can't you wait until the fair ends? I intend to be here at least three weeks, four if it seems profitable." The trader waved to a passing acquaintance. "We could ride south together. There are things even you have never seen and I'm the man to show them to you!"

The minstrel looked out upon the bustling grounds. There were still late arrivals but the field overflowed with tents and stalls.

"It is too bad the tournament was canceled," he remarked. "I might have stayed for that."

"It wouldn't have been the same without Sir Copago here to win everything," mused Galaro. "Why even you might have had a chance."

Guesare smiled at the jest, while recognizing its truth.

"It is possible," he said, "that young Donzalo and Habidros will ride with us."

"Ah." Galaro understood immediately why Guesare would wish to accompany them. "Would they travel further?"

"Donzalo has relatives in that region — his mother's people. He thought perhaps to visit them. Beyond that, who knows?"

"You have a habit of traveling 'beyond that,' Brother. All the way to Lorj once, as I remember."

"It could be a good place to see again. If Donni is willing, perhaps we'll sail across the straits."

"I've crossed those straits on occasion myself, Guesare, but never journeyed far inland. But then," he added, "I wasn't exactly supposed to be there."

~ ~ ~

"Would it not be better than having him underfoot here or at your uncle's keep?" asked Count Orgelo. "While he stays with us he could visit your mother's family. We're related, you know, by marriage. Probably in other ways, too, if one goes back far enough."

"Their lands lie close to yours?" I should know this already, Bolos told himself.

"They border us on our north. It is a small county and not a rich one. The current count would be a nephew of your late mother. So, a cousin." Orgelo fixed his gaze on the younger man. "Has he not visited here?"

Bolos shrugged. "If I were told it was so, I would believe it. I fear I never paid much attention to such matters.

"Be that as it may. I know that Donzalo does not particularly wish to remain here. He has been storing away his belongings and has moved into a small room near the stables. He even let his manservant go." But not his bodyguard was the thought that came to both men's minds.

"He may be safer, too, in County Arvaram," said Orgelo. "We are not friendly with Sharsh there — of this I am certain you are aware."

Yes, let his brother be someone else's problem for a time, thought Bolos. "If Sir Donzalo wishes it, he has my permission." Whether Sharsh or the man seated beside him had a part in his father's death, he would be glad to have both Donzalo and Orgelo far away.

"Will you come to the Midsummer bonfire tomorrow night?" Bolos asked his guest. "I think it is time to return cheer to our land."

"I shall try but fault me not should I fall asleep." Orgelo rose. "I bid you good night and good fortune, Count Bolos."

"And I to you, Count Orgelo."

Bolos looked around his father's office — *his* office. He should have more space, he thought, and he would never sleep in that tiny room upstairs. Maybe he should take a look at the rooms Donzalo had just vacated. Why his brother had chosen new quarters in a stable storeroom neither he nor anyone else in the keep could fathom.

## 4

Lareth felt he should speak of this to his sons and no others, for now. Whom else might he trust?

"The count was a threat to us, wasn't he sir?" asked Gawis.

"His son might have been," said the younger brother, Modareth, "had the marriage happened."

Lareth slowly shook his head. "It is unlikely that Copago would have ever posed a threat. Had he, we would have moved against him later rather than chancing chaos now.

"I fear," he continued, "that our Lord Radal had a hand in this."

Gawis knew Radal only as a presence in his father's court, a man feared by many but of unquestioned loyalty. Modareth, as a friend of the lord councilor's daughter, had a very different and more personal view of him.

"S — Sir," he said, his childhood stutter returning to haunt him at such moments, "wasn't the Lady Fachalana at County Rosam at the time of the murder?"

Indeed she was, thought Lareth, and fresh from showing her talent with a dagger here in the capital. But the king could not see Fachalana as a cold-blooded assassin. "I would think it most unlikely that she was involved," he replied.

He did wonder, though, why Radal would let his daughter be there at that time. Assuming the count's death *was* the work of Radal — that was not yet established.

And there was that girl who accompanied the lady, what was her name? Maresta. He must learn what his spies knew of her.

But he likewise doubted the slender actress was any sort of assassin.

"You are princes," King Lareth said to his sons, "and princes need advisers they can trust in all matters. If we can not trust Lord Radal, to whom should we turn?"

"Carrana's father seems trustworthy," offered Modareth, adding with an impish smile, "Certainly more so than my brother's father-in-law."

Gawis reddened but Lareth laughed aloud. "I am heartened that you can joke about the attempt on your life, my son. But the baron, trustworthy or no, is not a man I would ask for advice." He could picture the stout nobleman, a fellow both coarse and good-hearted, whose greatest ambition was to spend time in his vegetable garden. He might ask him for advice on the growing of cabbages.

"What of the man you yourself sent to County Rosam, Father? Is Lord Doufan to be trusted?" asked Gawis.

"Were he not many and many leagues distant he would be with us now in this room. I would expect a fuller report from his hand soon." Lareth turned to the windows, flung open to the summer sky. "Had we any sense we would all be out of the heat of Celatas by this time of year. I leave immediately for Mountain Keep."

He spoke to his eldest son, once again garbed in the king's own personal colors of green and white. "You must govern here for me, Gawis.

"Modareth, it is time that you and Carrana found the safety of a country keep. I have given orders for a twenty-man to escort you into the mountains."

~ ~ ~

Ros, despite being a year younger, stood almost as tall as his cousin. However, he did not talk nearly so much.

King could not decide which child he preferred, bouncing from one to the other.

"You should take the dog with you," said the Lady Lomela. "I fear its presence irritates my husband."

"Then we shall remove many irritants all at a once, my lady," Dame Janona replied. "What a head of hair your young Ros is growing!"

The boy's hair was thick, wavy, a dark brown that seemed almost red. "It is much the color of my father's hair," Lomela remarked, "when he was young." Ros favored his grandfather in many ways; his size, however, spoke of his father.

"Were he a horse, I might call it chestnut," observed Sir Paren.

"Behave yourself, Husband," chided the Lady Thara. "And that includes no dancing about the bonfire. You are far too old and fat for that."

"And too drunk, as well." admitted the knight. "Tonight, I think, will be made of memories of midsummers past." Paren deeply grieved yet for his brother.

"But once upon a time, wife of mine, we might both have thrown off our clothes and danced all night," he reminded her, with a wink.

Lomela tried not to picture that in her mind. These Lamans, so strait-laced and yet so given to their revelries and festivals!

"Remember," she told her three adult companions, "that we wish to rise early to visit the fair. It will be your only chance before you leave." She looked about. "Is anyone else joining us?"

"My husband and his mother chose to busy themselves for coming journeys," said Janona, "As did Grippo. We will see them not tonight." She smiled. "My Copago is not one for frivolity anyway."

He isn't, is he? thought Lomela. No dancing naked for the sober master of arms. Donzalo is really a bit like that, too — nearly as reserved but not so brusque.

"Does anyone know if Donzalo is coming?" she asked aloud.

"Donni is spending the evening with his friends from the Cuddon down at the fairgrounds," replied Paren. "I think a part of him yearns to return to that land."

They stood on the wide green beyond Castle Rosam's outer walls. Some days found sheep grazing here; some mornings saw duelists at their deadly game. This evening, a great crowd from keep and countryside and even the town surrounded a tower of firewood, soon to be the midsummer bonfire.

There was music about them, and laughter, and many blankets laid out on the green where groups and couples shared food and drink. Vendors wound their way through the throng, offering nuts and wine and prani. They could hear the voice of Saj, master of hounds, rising over the noise of the crowd as he made announcements.

"I wish Fachalana could have stayed for this," said the Lady Lomela, mostly to herself.

"There are many things for which we might wish, my lady," replied Janona. "Many things, indeed."

Lomela nodded in agreement. Where was Bolos in all this crowd? The man seemed adrift after the dual blows of his father's and daughter's deaths.

The festivities of this night, and tomorrow's Summer Feast, might help. And then the new count could fall into the routine of governing and daily life and, perhaps, forgetfulness.

Lady Lomela smiled to herself. If only things could be that easy!

~ ~ ~

"Your blond roots are showing, Maresta. Will you dye again?" Fachalana knew to address her friend by that name here; ever the actress, she found it easy to slip into whatever play in which she found herself cast.

"My dye is with our luggage, far away. I think I will let it grow out." Ansa peered into her hand-mirror. "Maybe a hat until then?"

"Or a wig." Fachalana grew suddenly serious. "How soon do you think we can leave? I must speak with the king."

"Fear not, my lady. I spoke to Sir Blen before you awoke and he says King Lareth is on his way here.

"How do you feel this morning? You were barely with us when we arrived."

Fachalana's father, on seeing her condition the previous evening, had immediately prepared a draught for her. The young woman had slept long and soundly.

"As though I were made of lead," replied Fachalana, "but my mind has cleared."

"The Lord Radal was very concerned for you. He said that you might have been lost forever in whatever realms you walked in your dreams." Ansa found there were tears in her eyes. "I would not want to lose you, Lana."

"I, my friend, would not have wished to remain in the places I visited. But I found a place where I could rest, a place all of silver." The place where she had first seen Donzalo. "I do not think I was supposed to be there but it became my sanctuary."

"Oh, Fachalana, give up these magics! Is it not enough to be both an admired actress and the best swordswoman in Celatas?"

"Those things are like the dye in your hair, Maresta. The real me will continue to show at the roots."

~ ~ ~

*A cup of wine may make me jolly*
*But two can turn me melancholy,*
*And taking three is simple folly*
*For I'll fall asleep, by golly!*

*I'll have one for my stomach's sake,*
*Though several more seems a mistake;*
*Too many cupfuls surely make*
*Anybody's tummy ache!*

"Aye, that's true," came a gruff voice from the darkness.

*Good food is certainly a sign*
*To pour another cup of wine,*
*So bring enough when we may dine*
*To fill up yours and fill up mine!*

Cups were lifted all around the campfire.

*A cup of wine just might enhance*
*The mood that leads us to romance;*
*But sometimes we make an advance*
*When we shouldn't take the chance!*

Guesare put down his rebec and raised his own goblet of wine in salute to his audience. There was much revelry that midsummer night, all through the grounds of the fair, as men — and, yes, more than a few women — relaxed and celebrated before their first chaotic day of selling on the morrow.

"Is that one of yours?" queried Galaro.

"Only in part, Brother. The words come from Donzalo's friend, Jobareth."

"The Nafal boy? I've done business with his family."

"From what he has told me, they would rather put you out of business," said Donzalo, "and establish safe trade routes in the south."

"And it will happen, one way or another. My guess is that the Coradeans will reoccupy at least some of their old holdings on the mainland and make life hard for an honest smuggler." Galaro thought a moment and continued. "But it's no ones land down on the south coasts now. Pirates and plunderers. Maybe some order would be a good thing."

Habidros slapped his scabbard. "I'd show them how to bring some order."

There were chuckles around the fire at that, and most of all from his two brothers. Galaro and Guesare, once enemies — or nearly so — had found that they had much in common and, in fact, liked each other. Both were amused by their brother's mix of bravado and naivety.

"It is the southern passes that more interest the Nafals," Donzalo pointed out. "Our friend Orgelo would want to have a say in that."

"We shall have a first-hand look at that part of the world soon," said Guesare, "and maybe more. Does anyone else here know a song? I'm tired of being the entertainment!"

"I need to stretch my legs and visit the latrine," spoke Donzalo, coming to his feet. "No, Habi, you don't have to come along." His bodyguard had risen to accompany him.

"I'd feel better if I did," he responded.

"As would I," added Guesare. "You still need protection, Donni, even here."

"I'll go with him," said Galaro. "I need to piss too. Watch out for the tent ropes," he warned Donzalo. "It's easy to trip over one in the dark."

Once they were beyond the fire's light, he added, "A couple of old mother hens. Need some time to yourself?"

"Ha, you are observant Sir Galaro. I don't get much privacy these days."

"With all the fires and folks wandering about here, it is probably as safe as walking a street in town. Maybe safer, for we traders take care of our own."

They did pass by many others in the night, some hurrying on errands, others seemingly strolling at random. Donzalo noted one tall vagabond with a great beard, who turned from them and slipped into the dark. He looked at his companion.

Galaro nodded. "Perdos. I would expect no trouble from him here."

"Looking for information, you would think?"

"Aye. It's a good place to find it."

"Then he'll have learned where we are headed, most likely."

"I'll tell Guesare about it later. He's in no danger now. The latrines are up ahead, to the left. It would have been quicker just to go piss in the river."

Donzalo's smile might not have been visible in the dark. "When you pack and leave they drain them into the Weldar anyway. Saves on having to dig new ones."

## 5

"My grandfather was born here. They changed the name to Grenethas in his honor."

Carrana nodded amiably. She knew this. What she wanted was to see their new home.

Modareth pointed toward a forested hill. "The chateau is up there." He had never visited but he had maps. "Greneth used it mostly as a hunting lodge after he took the crown."

"Does your father come here?"

"Not since he was young, he told me." He pointed again, up the single cobblestone street of what was called a city only out of politeness. "A few leagues up you would meet the old Southern Road and a few leagues more will take you to the Doram Pass. That is why there are garrisons nearby." Exactly how far a 'few leagues' was remained somewhat nebulous in the prince's mind.

"But we will have our own soldiers, won't we?"

"The twenty Father has sent with us and a small guard that always remains stationed here. Fear not, my love, even if we have no Lady Fachalana to protect us." He leaned down from his piebald stallion to kiss his wife, riding beside him in a horse litter.

The way up to their residence was short but steep. It was more fortified house than keep, though a low wall surrounded it, built of the rather soft limestone that underlay much of this country.

"That roof needs repair," Carrana whispered to the prince. "I'll wager it's worse inside."

"Then at least we shall keep busy this summer, my dear. Let's go see just what sort of job awaits us!"

~ ~ ~

Summer Feast was a festive occasion and Summer Fair was a festive place but Lomela was not in a festive mood. Her husband had fallen again into his old drunken ways last night.

She hardly blamed him. Life had dealt him heavy blows lately and a midsummer revelry was a good place to forget ones cares for a time.

This did not mean that she liked it in any way nor that it did not worry her.

Her party had left the keep early, eager to get the best deals at the fair. Only adults this time — Lomela and her faithful maid, Traspa, Janona and her mother-in-law, Sima, Sir Paren and his Thara, along with a couple of guardsmen to protect and to carry packages. On the road down they were met by Jobareth Nafal and, to the utter surprise of all, the ambassador Lord Doufan.

He rode with them as though he were but another old friend, smiling and making small jests. Before long, they felt an old friend was just what he was.

One advantage of being a countess was that the soldiers of ones husband could be expected to care for your horses while you wandered afoot. There were many such soldiers stationed about the Summer Fair.

Lesser personages had to entrust their mounts to the makeshift — and not inexpensive — corrals that sprang up near the fairgrounds.

They left their horses and entered the already bustling field. Fresh straw had been strewn between the pavilions, soon to be ground into the mud. This was yet another argument for an early arrival.

Nafal pointed to their left as they entered the grounds. "Galaro's booths are close — he arrived early and got a good spot. Donzalo may or may not be there."

But the ladies had already descended upon a jewelry stall in the opposite direction.

And Doufan was in earnest discussion with a vendor of crockery. "It appears that some of your wares have met with misfortune," said he, regarding a pile of shards behind the counter.

"Part of the cost of my business, m'lord," came the reply.

"Indeed," remarked the diplomat, "if things didn't break, there would be no potters." It was an old proverb and known to both men.

"Quite so, sir, though I prefer they break after I sell them!"

Lord Doufan turned to Nafal and whispered, "Cheap and crude, from somewhere upriver. Would that all his wares had not survived transit."

Jobareth nodded. "Yes, my lord. My family buys better just to ship our wine." There were markets that still preferred amphora to wooden cask.

"Ah, of course you would know something of pottery then. What is our group up to?"

The women had moved on to the next booth, followed by Sir Paren and the two soldiers.

"Cloth. I know they will take their time on that," said the younger man. "Shall we make our escape, my lord?"

"A most excellent idea, young sir. I assume someone sells refreshments in this metropolis of merchants."

"Come with me to my brother's pavilion and you may drink for free," said Guesare, coming up from behind them.

"Is Donzalo there?" asked Jobareth as they walked beside the Cuddonian.

"No, he went back to the keep to finish his packing. Sir Paren and all his company will depart early on the morrow and he must have his things ready for transport."

"You leave the same day, Sir Guesare?" asked the ambassador.

"Most likely. That depends on the whims of Count Orgelo."

"Orgelo is a man who bears watching," remarked Doufan, without further comment.

His companions needed none. They both thoroughly agreed.

Galaro was not one to deal in just one trade-good. A variety of items were spread through the tents and stalls occupied by his band, though different members of that band did have each his specialties. Galaro's own was weaponry.

"It is unfortunate," Lord Doufan said, "that the Lady Fachalana did not have the opportunity to view your wares."

"I feel unfortunate, sir," replied Galaro, "that I missed the opportunity to meet her. Tales of her exploits have reached my ears from several sources now.

Mayhap I can cross swords with her someday."

Guesare laughed loudly. "She would cut you to ribbons, Brother!" He had that on the best authority, that being the word of Ansa. "As would I, you know."

"I have little skill with the sword," stated Doufan. As oft, Jobareth had no idea whether the man's words were true. "But I do appreciate a fine gunne. Are these all you have?"

"All I have for sale, my lord. There is something here, however, that you might like to see."

He went to a chest near the rear of the tent and pulled forth a long slender object wrapped in rawhide and, within that, oiled cloth. Galaro held it out to them.

"A musket?" asked Jobareth.

"No, boy, a rifle," came Lord Doufan's correction, "and as pretty a one as ever I've seen." He carefully took it from the trader. "Siphic?"

Galaro nodded. "It has a wheel-lock to rival any that ever went into a pistol. And look here," he said, taking the weapon back. "It loads from the breech." The mechanism looked complicated but its use seemed simple — the ornate trigger guard became a crank that opened the weapon for loading.

"You already have a customer waiting for it?" asked Doufan. "A rather wealthy one, I would hazard."

"No, my lord," replied Galaro, "it is meant to be a gift." He handed it to Guesare. "For all that has ever passed between us, I wish this to be yours."

Another man might have protested; Guesare knew better and embraced his brother.

"Ah, customers," said Galaro, as Lomela and her party approached. The men — Sir Paren included — were already laden. "And a countess among them, if I am not mistaken. Welcome to our pavilion, Lady Lomela.

"Gentlemen," he continued, "why don't you leave your burdens here? I will have them sent up to the keep for you later."

"Your Galaro knows how to do business with the nobility," observed Doufan in a low voice. "He seems quite a remarkable man."

Jobareth smiled. "The whole family seems remarkable, my lord."

~ ~ ~

That was the last of it. What he wished to send with Sir Paren was crated and stowed in the wagons. What little he needed here was in his new quarters, where he would sleep tonight on a simple cot.

At first, that little room had seemed stifling. It was not overly hot, thanks to the thick castle wall and the rock floor, but too close and without ventilation, even if Donzalo left the massive door ajar. Then he bethought him of the secret passage that lay beneath the chamber. Opening the panel to it let in a stream of air to pass out through his door.

Probably bats, too, he thought. And it would not do to have the passage visible when his room was open to passers-by. Maybe he should just take a pallet down to the cave. It might be a most pleasant spot to sleep on a warm summer night.

Donzalo doubted that he would spend any more nights at Keep Rosam this summer. Where would his so-called destiny lead him? A memory of his Jola came to him, of the moments of contentment he had found in her cottage. His hand went to the wolf pin at his shoulder.

And what of the women who were now in his life? The Lady Fachalana intrigued him and, yes, attracted him. He would admit it. But all that, in itself, meant little.

There was Ansa. Had he fallen in love with her, nearly a year ago, before he found Jola? Could she ever regain that place in his heart now?

Or the first woman he had loved, with all the passion that comes of such a first love, his princess — Lomela. Had the fire died or did it only flicker low now? Might they burn bright again?

From the open doorway, Bolos watched his brother, rapt in his thoughts, unaware of his presence. Bolos wished Donzalo no harm but would be gladdened to see him ride away from County Rosam. He had concerns enough, already.

He spoke. "Greetings, Brother." He walked into the room and looked about. "I had considered moving my private quarters here. These are smaller, but you do have that window."

"I will miss the window," Donzalo allowed with a smile.

"You didn't have to abandon these rooms, Donni. We would have held them for you." Bolos shook his head. "Instead you choose quarters in the stables."

"I can be out of the way there, and ready to come or go quickly." He looked into Bolos's eyes and continued earnestly, "I doubt, my brother, that I shall ever truly live here again. Best I move."

"Well, these rooms will probably remain empty a while. I have decided to take grandmother's old apartment."

"Ah. As Father intended."

Bolos nodded. "I wish you nothing but good fortune on your journeys, Brother, and do expect you to return to us. Maybe you'll be willing to take decent rooms then!" He chuckled at his own remark."Be a good ambassador for us to our neighbors, eh? And know that I do intend to name you as Uncle Paren's heir. If that is what you want."

He suspected that it was not.

## 6

Copago watched the little train pass out through the gates, his wife, his daughter, his mother, aye, and even the dog, off with Sir Paren and Lady Thara to take up residence in their keep. His own commission at Castle Rosam had ended yesterday. There was no more to hold him here.

The captain of Count Orgelo's troop came and stood silently beside him. He knew no proper words but did know the knight's heart was breaking.

Turning to him, Sir Copago spoke in his accustomed calm and even voice. "Is it time to go, Captain?"

"Nay, sir, the count is not yet ready. I would hazard an hour or two."

Copago nodded. He looked at his comrade's breastplate and asked a question he had at times before considered asking. "Why do the men of Aravaram wear that black-painted hardware? Is it not hot on a sunny day?"

"Isn't all armor hot?" returned the fellow. "Sir Sorsen claims it prevents rust but I think he just likes the look of it."

"Yes, that is Sorsen, isn't it?" He looked again toward the gates but there was nothing to be seen. Even the dust of the road had settled. "I prefer a good shine on my armor. It is more military."

"And a better target for a musketeer," replied the captain.

"I see it rather as a deterrent," opined Copago.

"Ha, I can see why our Sorsen likes you, Sir Copago. The two of you might argue armaments all day!"

"I can think of worse pastimes."

~ ~ ~

"You have spoken with your father, my lady?"

"I have. And do not call me my lady when we fence. My master said all men become equals when they hold swords."

"Until they cross them. I have heard that one," replied Blen. "When we cross swords you very much become my better."

"There are many in your company," spoke Ansa, lounging against a wall while the two practiced swordsmanship. "Tell me, sir, how does she compare with Donzalo? I heard that you two exercised frequently."

"He is certainly far my superior. Let's stop and have some water." He dropped his point to the stone floor. "Whether he is better than Lady Fachalana, I am not qualified to judge."

Lady Fachalana glared at him for using her title.

"What? Shall I call you Lana as does Maresta?"

"Just Fachalana. It is not difficult, man."

Blen bowed to her. "Very well, Fachalana. I will say that Donzalo has a prodigious reach to his advantage."

Ansa had poured them tumblers of cold water, always readily available here in the mountains, as they approached her. "Fachalana has a pretty good reach herself," she remarked, handing them their drinks.

The lady laughed. "My father has warned me that I reach too far," she said. "But how else does one learn the length of ones arms?"

"An inch at a time," responded Sir Blen with great seriousness. "I must agree with the Lord Radal."

"And even one inch can give the advantage," added Ansa.

"Until someone else has an inch more," retorted Fachalana. She drank deeply and turned to Blen. "What do you intend to tell the king about Maresta?"

"Mostly the truth. That is, that she has served both you and the Princess Lomela with her actions. Is there more I should tell him?"

"Only what you know will serve quite well enough," Ansa said, "and we shall leave any secrets I might have out of it! Even so, it will not help my career one bit."

Blen would assume she meant on the stage; Fachalana recognized that she was referring to her life as a spy.

"Then find a nice boy and retire," suggested the Lady Fachalana. Maybe the one right in front of you, she said to herself.

~ ~ ~

Over the river before noon. That's not so bad, felt Guesare.

He and Habidros had been assigned a spot near the dusty rear of this column, ahead only of the baggage, while Donzalo and Sir Copago rode on either side of the count. The three seemed to have much to talk about.

He considered the thought that Orgelo regarded the two Cuddonians as baggage too. They would not be in his train were it not for Donzalo.

What the three men ahead were sharing were their remembrances of the late Count Borrago.

"The count was greatly pleased by the way Donzalo matured this past year. He very much loved this over-sized son of his."

"Of the three of us, you may have loved Father best," asserted Donzalo. "And he could never conceal his pride in you."

"Then, it would seem," Orgelo mused, "that the current count was his least favorite."

Neither was sure how to answer that. "No, that's all right," said their host, holding up a hand. "I know that Bolos long vexed his father with his drunkeness and sloth. He made strides in this past year as well, didn't he?"

"That he did, sir," allowed Copago.

"But he could and can still be thoroughly unpleasant, " added Donzalo. His half-brother had to nod in agreement. "He is my brother and I love him anyway."

"And I will truthfully admit that I do not," stated the former master of arms. "I will also say that I feel no anger toward him."

"That is a good start," said the count, "for your new life. I can not guarantee this, lad, but I would lay odds that Sorsen will name you his master of arms. If not, I can promise you a captaincy in my own troops."

"I thank you, my lord, again." They were making excellent time along the west banks of the Weldar. Here, the way was nearly as good as the Great Road on the other side of the river. "I have never traveled far south before."

"Nor have I," added Donzalo. "Father would not permit me to study in Morparas."

"With good reason," snorted Sir Copago. "A city of thieves and whores!"

Orgelo laughed loudly. "'Tis not so bad, my strait-laced friend. I do a fair amount of business in the city and you may have to travel there from time to time."

He turned his eyes toward Donzalo. "You are the more traveled, now, aren't you? All the way to the upper Cuddon, I've heard."

"Yes, my lord. I would have visited Oles as well, if my traveling companions had permitted."

"You missed little there. I visited when my father was count, on a mission of reconciliation to the pontifex. It ended not well."

"I've always found plenty to keep me busy at home," stated Copago. "Why seek trouble in other lands?"

Donzalo and the count exchanged expressions of amusement. "You, my boy," said Orgelo, "are far too much like your father."

"Thank you once more, my lord," said Copago, bowing from the saddle.

~ ~ ~

Perdos had shaved. Not just trimmed his lengthy beard back to its old accustomed length, but shorn it entirely. It was a break with the life he had been living — a symbolic gesture, of sorts, though he would never have thought of it in such terms. He just felt he should start afresh.

His face had not been without whiskers since he left the village of his birth, a little village north of Oles, near the Muram borders. He felt rather naked.

He had learned enough at the fair, back at Ros-town. Guesare would be traveling south on the west side of the river, with a sizable body of men. He would do the same on the east, by himself.

Surely, the minstrel had no intentions of staying at Tod-ford, at Count Orgelo's court. Sooner or later he would leave, quite possibly with his brother Galaro, when the trader came south again. Perdos

116

had no quarrel with Galaro and had parted amiably with the man, but he would not let him come between him and Guesare. Hadn't he said they were unfriendly to each other, anyway?

South he rode. He might stop by the inn where he had wintered, had he the time. He had little enough money left to pay for even a drink, though.

Then, cross and head for Todmouth. News from upriver always found its way there and, too, Galaro was likely to pass through.

Perdos could think of no better plan and perhaps there was none.

~ ~ ~

Someone was shaking Blen awake. "Wha — who is there?" he demanded, groping for his dagger.

"Ssshhh! It's Fachalana."

"Lady Fachalana?" He realized he was quite naked, having always slept so. The knight wrapped himself in a sheet and rose to light a taper from the still-glowing coals on his hearth. Even in midsummer the nights were cool enough at Mountain Keep for a fire.

The lady was dressed for riding. "I need your help, Sir Blen," said she.

His placed his candle on the table and sat down on his bed. "Speak, my lady."

"I have just learned that the king is a day away on the road. I must speak to him before he arrives. It is an urgent message and for his ears only. Will you ride with me to meet him?"

The knight suddenly felt a great need to use his chamberpot. Ride with her? "What of, uh, Maresta?" he asked, as his mind became less cobwebbed.

"She will remain and cover for us. If you come not with me, I will ride alone."

"The king — yes, my lady, I will ride with you. Meet me in the stables in ten minutes."

Fachalana hurried away from Sir Blen's quarters, stimulated by thoughts of action. The sight of the handsome and not at all clothed young knight had also provided a certain stimulation of its own. The Lady Fachalana was in too great a rush to sort all that out right then.

## 7

Business was good. On this third day of the fair, the crowds had less-
ened — albeit, not by much — and now many traders were getting
down to the business that truly brought most of them here, the
exchange of goods that they would carry out into all corners of Lama,
aye, and beyond, for resale.

That business could remain brisk through the entire month of
Summer Fair, as new wares flowed in. There was always a question of
whether to leave sooner and get a jump on the competition or remain
longer and find new bargains.

"Captain." Sir Galaro looked up to see his second, his one good
eye squinting into the morning sun. "The count is here."

Well, it was to be expected that Bolos would visit sooner or later.
"On the grounds?"

"Still at the gates, getting his men and mounts sorted out. I reckon
he'll be wandering through before long."

"Let's hope he isn't as stingy as his father was." Reports did not
make Galaro optimistic about that. "I think I'll wander myself and go
get a look at him." The burly Cuddonian rose and strolled toward the
fairground entrance.

He didn't think he had seen the new count this year, save at
Borrago's funeral. Had he? Anyway, Bolos had visited the fair the last
couple years when Galaro did business there, so he was acquainted
with the man. He had sold him some trinkets to give to one dalliance
or another.

There he was, slimmer than he remembered him in years past.
Less ostentatious, too, in an almost too subdued gray tunic. Around
him, his men were resplendent in their green and black uniforms and
burnished armor. He was hectoring one of them about something at
the gate.

Then there was chaos.

It took a second for Galaro to realize what had happened, to see
why Count Bolos's men suddenly surrounded him, swords turned
outward. There in a gate post still quivered a crossbow bolt.

The Cuddonian realized later that he had heard the thud of its strike. He also realized he had acted instinctively but wisely by immediately turning and walking swiftly back to his pavilion. The scene of an assassination attempt was one place it would not do to linger.

This would probably ruin business for the rest of the day. Galaro suddenly wished he did not have an assortment of crossbows among his goods.

~ ~ ~

The girl had settled down some. That was good. She was out riding with Sir Blen, he had been told. He did not trust Blen in many regards but he was certainly a safe and trustworthy companion for his daughter.

Radal wondered if Fachalana's recent near-madness had left her stronger. There had been no evident relapse nor requests for more sleeping draughts.

Now, there were other concerns. He had known the king must come eventually. How would he deal with his liege when Lareth arrived? Time was short but he had already taken the next steps in his plans.

The king could not stop them. Even if Radal himself were dead, too many things had been set in motion. He must trust in them to play out the way he had intended, to fulfill his design.

And he must trust Fachalana now to find her own way. Only the gods knew if he would be able to guide her further and he would not ask them. Radal had little trust in gods.

Certainly not in any he had ever met.

He would do what he could when Lareth came. Perhaps he could even sway his king to his viewpoint. Even so, his old friend would never again trust him.

But Lareth would not have him executed nor, probably, even imprisoned. An exile, far from power, might more likely be his fate. Radal would not mind that.

Indeed, he would mind little so long as Donzalo Rosam ceased to exist.

~ ~ ~

Four soldiers rode forth from the head of the column. They did not like the look of these two travelers speeding toward them. One held up a hand, calling for them to halt.

"Who rides?" he demanded.

"Sir Blen and the Lady Fachalana. We bear an urgent message for the king," replied the knight.

The name of Fachalana was known to them. The soldiers looked at her with a great deal of interest. "Go inform the captain," said their leader to one of them. The man wheeled his steed and galloped back.

The captain, wearing the king's colors of argent and green, and a handful more of men reached them shortly. This officer knew the Lady Fachalana. "My lady," he said, bowing from the saddle, "what is this message?"

"It is for King Lareth's ears only," she replied, with a great deal of assumed authority. "Tell him. He will want to hear it."

The man hesitated only a second, then nodded. "Follow me," he ordered.

By that time the column of men and horses had reached them. The captain rode close to the king and spoke to him. Lareth shielded his eyes against the morning sun coming over the mountains and looked in the direction of Fachalana and Blen. Then he nodded and gave the man an order.

"Come with me," said the captain, when he returned to the pair. "The lady only," he added when Sir Blen started forward.

The king's men fell back to a discreet distance while the Lady Fachalana rode alongside their liege. Blen saw a look of astonishment cross his face. What secret message could she have been bearing?

Then the king looked toward him and asked a question. Fachalana shook her head and answered with a smile. Her smile was returned by the monarch. The knight quite rightly surmised that Lareth wanted to know if he were in on whatever secret the lady was conveying to him.

Then the king beckoned to him.

"I thank you, Sir Blen," said Lareth when the knight was beside him, "for once again serving well your king. Better than you know, this time, or perhaps ever will know."

"The Lady Fachalana asked and I acted, sir. Whatever service I may have performed was at her bidding."

Now that this so-important message had been delivered, Blen bethought himself of a question. "Should we hurry back to the Keep, sire, or ride on with you?"

The king turned his eyes to Fachalana. "What think you, my lady?"

"We should ride back immediately and swiftly. No one there knows we came to you nor should they." The king understood that she spoke of her father. Blen guessed something of the same.

"Then let us ride, my lady. We can be back hours before the king arrives. Maybe even in time for lunch!"

Blen had, of course, had no time for breakfast.

~ ~ ~

To Guesare's surprise, he had been asked to ride with Count Orgelo this day. The count was much interested in his travels, and their talk, more than once, turned to his brother Galaro.

He doubted that he told the man much of anything he didn't already know but he enjoyed telling his many tales. By the time they stopped for the evening, Guesare realized he had learned much himself, especially of his brother's exploits.

The men set up targets that night and held matches at archery. The minstrel let loose a few arrows with a borrowed longbow, but with no more than decent results. The recurved eastern bow was his weapon and he knew he could best any man here at its use from horseback.

The minstrel was amused that his brother Habidros proved a most wretched archer. "I've not touched a bow in years, " the man offered as excuse. "Give me a gunne," he growled, "and I'll show you a few things."

At the end it came down to Sir Copago and, to the surprise of Donzalo and the Cuddonians but none others there, Orgelo. The count had been a famed archer in his youth and still had the needed steady eye and hand. Eventually, he avenged his son's unhorsings at the hands of Copago.

"Sir Guesare," he called, "bring forth that rifle of which we have heard."

"I have not yet fired it, my lord, and know not its capabilities." He rummaged in one of the carts before drawing forth the carefully wrapped firearm.

Donzalo had heard of the weapon but not seen it. He found himself greatly fascinated by its mechanism once Guesare had it out and wiped down for action. There was great interest, as well, from Orgelo and his men.

The minstrel carefully loaded it and closed the breach, silently saying a prayer to the goddess Rema that it would remain closed as it was supposed to. Then he primed and spanned it, and took aim at one of the targets.

"Did I hit it?" he asked after the smoke cleared. A man who had run to the target pointed to a spot near its outer edge.

"May I?" asked Habidros, taking the rifle from his hands and a swab to its barrel. "It's rather a small bore, isn't it?" He prepared the weapon for firing, and then turned and walked twenty paces further from the target before taking aim.

This time a hole near the bullseye was pointed out. "It shoots well, Brother," remarked Sir Habidros, returning the rifle to its owner.

"You must have a scabbard made for it, my boy," insisted Lord Orgelo, "and a befitting one. Such a weapon should hang at your saddle, not be bundled away in a baggage cart."

"Indeed, my lord. And I think my brother needs to give me lessons in marksmanship!"

~ ~ ~

The reeve of Mountain Keep came forth to greet his king. This was the man entrusted with its everyday operation, who sent out patrols to keep the King's Pass clear and aid travelers at all times of the year.

He had much to tell his monarch but Lareth would not take the time. "Later. I must see Lord Radal. Accompany me, sir."

It was not yet dusk though the sun had dropped behind the mountains, cooling the air. Soon, the two stood before the ebony door of Radal's tower. "Await me," he said, and entered.

The king was immediate and straight-forward with his accusation. "You ordered the assassination of Borrago."

"I will not deny it, my lord," replied the sorcerer in an even voice. "I did what I believed necessary."

"Against my express orders. Radal, you know I can not have this. You may no longer serve as my lord councilor nor have you any other authority."

The dark nobleman bowed his head. "As expected, my king. Yet I would do it again," he added, with more vehemence.

"I know you would. But I tell you now that we will not again attempt to harm Donzalo Rosam. New information has come to me that changes our relationship with him completely."

"Might I know this secret, my lord?"

"No, Radal, you may not. I fear you would use it against him rather than as I wish. I am sorry it has come to this."

"What has come, has come. We must make the most of it," stated the sorcerer.

"So we must," answered King Lareth, turning to the door. "Pray to any gods you may have left that I can make something of this."

Once outside, Lareth issued orders to the reeve. "I wish you to set a guard at the Lord Radal's door, and make it a strong one. He is not to leave his tower.

"And have the Lady Fachalana and her companion come to my apartments for supper. Not Sir Blen, the girl."

He could speak with Blen later.

## 8

Who would profit from his death? That question pointed to a whole different group of suspects than had Borrago's assassination.

Surely Donzalo wouldn't be trying to clear a path to his title. Yet who else might want both him and his father dead? No, Bolos could not believe that.

Copago seemed an even less likely suspect.

But Donzalo's friend, the trader Galaro, was at the fairgrounds. With a selection of crossbows. He must have his agents keep an eye on the man.

Orgelo wouldn't mind having Donzalo as count, would he, or as regent for his nephew? The two had seemed altogether too friendly lately.

He hoped Sir Corgos would accept his offer of a position. Such a man was needed here. Jak was useless, save as sergeant to his personal guard.

Bolos took another sip from the flagon before him. There would be more flagons before the night was through, but no answers.

~ ~ ~

Ansa had been apprehensive when invited into Lord Radal's presence. The king of Sharsh made her even more so.

As soon as his young guests were seated at the table, one on his either hand, Lareth asked, "How much does your friend know, Lady Fachalana?"

"Everything, sire. She was my, um, liaison to your daughter last year."

The king laughed at that. "Your spy, you mean. I have learned much of Maresta lately. But not her origins." He gave Ansa a most disconcerting look. "That may remain your secret, if you wish."

"Th — thank you, my lord," she mumbled.

"Now, my dear, " he said, turning again to Fachalana, "you must have an official family name to go with your title."

"Sire, I would use that of my grandfather and vindicate his legacy."

"So, Lady Fachalana, the Viscountess Ildoram. I would be pleased to honor the memory of General Ildor." He gave her a long look, long in part because the servants were hovering close as they placed food and drink before them. He raised his filled goblet. "And I drink to his memory. How much do you know of the man?"

"My father never speaks of him, sir. I only know that he was a mercenary from Lorj who served King Greneth."

"Yes, from the south of the island and therefor with a Partanacan heritage. To be honest, I know not whether he served Coradean or Partanacan causes before he fled, nor know I why he fled. But he landed here and rose in my father's service. He married well, too, or so it seemed.

"You may not know that his wife, your grandmother, had gifts like your father's, and knew not how to harness them. As she grew madder and more dangerous, it weighed on Ildor and, I think, led him to become foolhardy. After he fell in battle, Radal cared for her but she, too, soon passed. Some whispered that she leaped from her tower window one night.

"My father saw the mother in the son. That is why he banished him." Lareth shook his head slowly. "Perhaps Greneth saw correctly. I fear for Radal's mind and soul."

His soul is long lost, Fachalana said to herself. I've known that, haven't I?

"You understand why I have placed him under guard, don't you?"

Fachalana had visited her father earlier and seen the guardsmen, but Radal would not speak of them to her.

"I believe so, my lord. What will become of my father?"

"When things are sorted out, retirement to a country estate. That is my hope, anyway."

"That is — kind of you, sir."

"I owe him much. As I do his daughter."

Back in the Anian court, the man would be garroted by now, thought Ansa. But she held her tongue and picked at the meal set before her. Was this chicken hiding beneath the sauce?

126

"Now I would ask another favor of his daughter. I have sent Prince Modareth and his bride to my father's old estate in Dor." The king raised his cup. "This wine comes from our vineyards there."

Ansa sniffed at the golden liquid in her goblet. She felt she would have preferred tea.

"My ladies, will you travel there and visit with them? It is not that distant a journey, though rugged if one follows roads near the mountains.

"Oh, and I shall send Sir Blen with you."

"Our luggage will never catch up with us at this rate, sir," said Lady Fachalana, "but we would be most willing to catch up with your son and the Lady Carrana.

She raised her cup. "To the journeys that come!"

~ ~ ~

There were only burnt ruins where the inn had once stood. Perdos stood mute, numb. Who had done this?

A man was walking toward him from the river. A somewhat stout man, a somewhat familiar man. Hendel. He remembered him from Keep Rosam.

The man did not seem to remember him, however. Perhaps his lack of beard could be credited for that. Or perhaps Hendel had simply never paid any attention to the soldier.

"Knew you the innkeepers, sir?" asked the man.

"I did," replied Perdos. "I would have counted them friends." He turned to Hendel. "What happened?"

"A band of marauders. Murdered them both, though perhaps not quickly enough." Hendel spat. "I curse the man who led them and I curse the fact that I know him. Sojel is his name, a mercenary out of Mura."

"Sojel," Perdos softly repeated to himself. "What brings you here, sir?"

"I left Todmouth a few days ago, growing, um, unhappy with my employment there. I am a cook," he offered. Perdos made no comment.

127

"My home town lies but a little upriver," said the man, gesturing in that general direction, "so I crossed here thinking to visit. Instead I found this. They murdered the guards down at the ferry too, I hear, and the current ones are very edgy. Even with their numbers doubled.

"Though I do mourn their loss of life, I recognized an opportunity and set up a little stall down close to Weldar where I might sell meat pies and such to passers-by."

Perdos nodded. "I may come down later to sample your wares. Could you leave me alone for a time?"

"Certainly, good sir," said the cook, with genuine sympathy, and headed back toward the ferry crossing.

When the man was well away, the knight picked his way through the burnt timbers to the great fireplace, standing yet. Might it still be here? he wondered.

He pulled out a stone. He had seen the innkeeper pull the same stone on occasion and made note of it. It had been the man's hiding place for his cash. Perdos had just enough honor to leave that be.

There was no point in that now, though, was there? Yes, there were the coins, tucked away in bags. Three bags, that crumbled at his touch. The heat must have done that, Perdos thought.

He filled his saddlebags with the loose money and headed toward the river and a meat pie.

~ ~ ~

The King's Pass was what Greneth had officially named it but most still called it the North Pass. Now Fachalana, Ansa, and Blen rode down from the pass toward Sharsh, accompanied by the four soldiers King Lareth had assigned them.

They would follow the Royal Road for some way and then turn left, southward, and follow roads that paralleled the ridges of the Zadcelam all the way to Dor.

Blen did not particularly like this plan of action. He would rather be back to Lama than accompanying these two girls. They seemed girls today, anyway, chattering gaily as they rode along. He knew they were two quite competent young women.

The knight liked them. It had been grudging at first and the knowledge that he was being shut out of many of their secrets did not help. But they had grown on him, even the sometimes difficult and undeniably dangerous Lady Fachalana.

Blen did not doubt for one moment that Ansa was quite dangerous as well, despite appearances.

Well, he had no orders to remain with them at Grenethas, only to get them there. It would be easy enough to cut back into Lama through the southern pass, the Doram Pass, the other major route through the mountains. That could be an interesting experience, too.

~ ~ ~

Lord Radal climbed to the highest chamber of his tower. One of his small messengers awaited him, bearing news from his agent at the Rosam embassy. It took little talent to deal with such messengers and that was what the boy had — a little talent.

The faked assassination attempt had gone off much as planned, though the intention had been to strike one of the soldiers, not a post. That did as well. Lareth could not put a halt to those plans by locking him in here; still, the sorcerer might operate more efficiently were he elsewhere.

Three nights ago had he called. To the Lofty Mountains had he called, beyond the mighty River Siph, beyond the plains of the Anians.

To the dragons had he called. He felt now the rush of wind that arose from mighty wings. He saw the eyes aglow in the darkness and smelt the stench of its fires. His steed had come and he would ride it.

Lord Radal fled on the wings of night.

# OF CROSSINGS: THE EIGHTH TALE

## 1

Pol was not happy about this assignment. Was it Jobareth Nafal's idea to send him across Lama in the worst heat of summer?

Yes, probably.

And with that cart, it would take more than two weeks to reach the mountains. Mountain Keep would have been further but the roads to that destination were better.

He and the man at arms who accompanied him — a good Sharshite fellow and eager to be home — checked the map they had been given. They had followed the way they all knew well, the road by which he and the soldier and the two in the wagon had come into the heart of Lama, for some distance before turning due west toward the mountains and Doram Pass. Pol had been told there was a good road. It was rough, the red dirt rutted from traffic and summer downpours, but passable.

Murbalana was complaining again. "Did you put up with that all the way here?" he asked his companion.

"We did, Sergeant. Many a day I envied Doo his deafness." He had not told the man to address him as sergeant. That must have been Nafal's doing, too.

They had been all set to head off to Mountain Keep when the messenger came with this change of plan. Cross at the southern pass and find the ladies summering in Dor. Pol had heard of Dor but had never been there.

He was contemptuous of its wine, having been raised in Arolin where they produced the finest vintages in the world. Everyone he had ever known from his home province assured him it was so.

Pol looked toward the cloud-filled sky. There would be afternoon rains again. "I hope there are decent inns along this route," he muttered, "with decent wine."

His companion nodded his agreement.

~ ~ ~

"I ask this not for myself nor even for Lord Bolos, but for your friend Copago. He should have a worthy successor at his post."

"Would you order me to go, sir?"

"Never. It is for you and your wife to make this decision."

"Very well," said Sir Corgos, "I shall put it to Tiana." He leaned back in his chair. "I do like it here, Sir Paren."

"Lad, I have seen that you sometimes grow bored. There is little to challenge you in my keep," Paren observed. "I am sure your Tiana has seen it as well.

"You never speak of it but I know you have seen much of the world in your young life."

"Young? My lord, for a soldier I am already something of an old man. Older than Copago by half a decade." He sighed. "It was more than time to leave such a life."

"That it was. But you needn't bury yourself here in the backwoods. You know," the reeve continued, "Tiana might like life at Castle Rosam."

"Indeed, Sir Paren. But might that be a good thing or a bad one?"

~ ~ ~

"Why isn't the pass here used more?" asked Carrana. "It seems more convenient than going further north."

"I think," replied her husband, "it is because there isn't much of anything on the other side. The King's Pass is the gate to Oles and the Siphic cities beyond.

"Also, I hear it is a longer and rougher path. There are many ways through the mountains, in truth, but the others are not very practical for anyone but goats and smugglers."

"We should ride up and look at it some time, Modi."

"I fear it will only look like mountains. Besides," said the prince, "I am not certain you should be traveling at all."

"Pooh. It is nothing. My mother attended a ball the night before I was born."

"And danced with every man there. Yes, my dear, you have told me before." Modareth turned an ear toward the ceiling. "There is another leak somewhere. I can hear it dripping."

"I hope we can get them all fixed before the Lady Fachalana arrives."

"She wouldn't mind them, Carrana. Indeed, she might be inclined to get up on the roof and fix them herself." A courier had arrived only that morning, informing them of the viscountess' impending visit.

"I wonder about this Sir Blen who will accompany her. Her friend Maresta I know, of course."

"The actress?" asked Carrana. "I hope she isn't as wicked as her stage roles!"

"Oh no, my dear, she's quite a sweet, guileless girl and wouldn't hurt a fly, I am sure."

~ ~ ~

Count Bolos paced back and forth in his wife's sitting room.

"So the Maresta who accompanied Lady Fachalana is one and the same as the Posena who came here as a spy?" asked Bolos. "Why was I not told — or my father?"

"It was unimportant, my husband. She was only here incognito at Fachalana's request."

"And I learn of it through gossip picked up by my agents. What am I to think when you keep such secrets from me?"

If only he knew what secrets I do keep, thought Lomela. "That I do not wish to bother you with trifles, sir."

"Humph. I have little trust in all these foreigners, be they from Sharsh or the Cuddon." He paused, abashed by his own poor choice of words. "Not all Sharshites, my lady. I do trust you.

"But I know not who else to trust and who to suspect. It must be admitted that the way this woman and your friend fled was most suspicious."

Princess Lomela diverted the subject. "A few days ago I might have told you not to trust my father. I have reason to suspect that might be changing."

"Indeed? Have you your own network of spies, my dear?"

"One might say that, Husband. I call them my friends in Sharsh who write to me with all the latest news. Those are the very best sorts of spies, for they do not know that they are." She smiled at the count. "You will hear this soon, anyway, but there has come a break between the king and Lord Radal. The sorcerer has been stripped of power."

"And you learned this from whom?"

"His daughter, Bolos. The Lady Fachalana."

~ ~ ~

Lord Doufan sat in a tavern near the Ros-town docks, nursing an ale and watching all that happened around him.

He became bored in the embassy. Indeed, there was little for him to do with the efficient legate tending to most of the necessary day-to-day diplomatic work.

The ambassador knew he could be of use at Castle Rosam but the count would not see him. The man seemed distrustful of all strangers, hiding behind walls built of stone and of wine.

Therefor, Doufan rode. Though he had chosen to give the impression otherwise on his trip here, the nobleman was quite comfortable on horseback. Sometimes he simply rode alone in the countryside, seeing what there was to see. At other times he would make his way down to Ros-town and visit one tavern or another, learning more of these Lamans among whom he must, for a while, live.

When he chose, he could be a popular fellow at those taverns, always ready with the right words and a bit of money. Often, as today, he chose to observe instead, keeping to himself.

"What word, Grandfather?" asked a young woman who sat down across from him. He did not mind that the whore saw him as an old man; it was the impression he intended to project.

And he *was* old enough to be her grandfather, after all.

"None you would care to hear, my dear," he replied. After a moment, she moved on.

It was probably dangerous to be in such places, not that he was in any way defenseless. He had all the training of a Sharshite noble in sword and dagger, and carried a well-concealed brace of pistols as well. Lord Doufan was not nearly so innocuous as he chose to appear.

This place, low-ceilinged and dark, was favored by stevedores and raftsmen. Rough men but honest, for the most part. He might be able to defend himself but he would not care to indulge in a fist-fight with one of these burly fellows.

Nafal, perhaps, saw into him — as far as he had let him, anyway. The boy was smart and an excellent administrator, but he would never be able to do what Doufan did. Yet he might well take Lord Radal's place one of these days while faceless diplomats such as the Lord Doufan were forgotten.

That was all to the good.

## 2

Across the wide Laman valley the dragon had flown, over the mighty Weldar and toward the high hills of the Cuddon. They would have passed near Castle Rosam but Radal could not see it in the dark.

There was a place, a small keep, in the rugged central highlands, east and some south of the River Abam, that the sorcerer knew. He knew it was empty for it had been occupied by the deceased and inept wizard Sabatare.

It would do as his new base of operations.

His mount was slowly descending toward the tower, practically a ruin, its great wings riding subtle winds that rose along the faces of the steep, scrub-covered hills. Radal could see the dragon clearly now in the morning light, seemingly a large beast at first glance but mostly all wing and slender, snake-like body. The big dragons did not fly; their bulk could not be supported by any wings.

He had paid dearly for this transport. What did that matter when he had already bartered away all that was Radal years ago? With his extinction would come peace and any torments before that were meaningless.

The sorcerer longed, these days, to fall into that great darkness.

He alit from the worm in an unkempt space before the crumbling walls. The beast eyed him for a few seconds — hungrily, perhaps? — before launching itself into the still morning air.

Radal thought of all he had left behind in Sharsh. He could never return now, not go into a quiet retirement, never have Fachalana's children playing about their grandfather, unaware of who he once had been. He must trust his daughter to find her way, to give him those grandchildren he would not see.

All this he did for her, now. He knew that Donzalo was entwined in her fate, as he had been in her sister's. Radal could not let the man live. He could not lose both Fachalana and Jola.

He would need a horse, wouldn't he? Radal turned toward the doors of Sabatare's keep — the magics that barred them were easily swept away — and went do the things he must do.

~ ~ ~

He knew his old circle was not trustworthy. But where might Gawis find new advisers?

The bureaucrats aiding him with all the small details of governing in his father's absence were useful men, but not ones he would take into his confidence. He needed someone at his right hand, someone loyal to him only, as Lord Radal had so long served his father.

Yes, that was ending badly now but the dark nobleman had been faithful many years. It was madness that drove him these days, wasn't it? Not malice toward the king.

The sorcerer perhaps did not see it as betrayal at all.

Gawis toyed with a paperweight on his desk. It was dark green glass, blown at one of the shops right here in Celatas, in a fanciful fish shape. They did good work with glass here. Celatas could rival any city in that industry.

There was his brother. He knew Modareth was smart. But would he be loyal to his brother? The two had never been close — too much difference in age, not to mention temperament, in the siblings born to different mothers. He might ask the boy's advice but doubted he would ever trust him with his secrets.

It seemed the only one to whom he could unburden himself was his wife. Mara could be insightful; after all, she had grown up in the great imperial court of Partanaca and knew the ways of power. Even if she shunned them, herself.

He eyed the stack of papers before him. Why did they all need his signature? Prince Gawis took one from the top of the pile and began reading.

~ ~ ~

Ansa was eyeing a small harp placed on a table in the library.

"You play the harp, my lady?" asked Modareth. "It was my mother's instrument but I fear I have no skill on it myself."

She ran a finger across the strings. It was much out of tune. "My brother taught me, when I was a girl." Ansa looked up at the prince. "He is a minstrel, my lord."

For a few moments, she twisted the wooden tuning pins and then sang, in a high, clear voice.

*Moon of silver, sun of gold,*
*I who was young now grow old.*
*Daylight dims, night grows cold,*
*Should I fear death, I who was bold?*

*Life is short, forever is long,*
*I tried to do right, often did wrong.*
*Will is weak, wine was strong,*
*I would forget the words to my song.*

*Moon of silver, queen of night,*
*I knew you once, grown full and bright,*
*And madly I danced, by your light,*
*But those who danced with me fled from sight.*

*Last fading stars, by dawn swept away,*
*I, as you, may no longer stay.*
*Yet you return, come end of day;*
*Where I might go, I can not say.*

*Every road walked, every tale told;*
*All I then loved I could not hold.*
*Sun of morning, spun of gold,*
*I who was young have grown old.*

"I didn't know you could sing, Maresta!" exclaimed the Lady Fachalana.

"None of my roles ever called for it," she answered.

"Our Maresta surprises me anew each day," spoke Sir Blen, from a chair in the corner.

Prince Modareth rose from the divan where he rested with his wife. "I must have those words written down, Lady Maresta. Did your brother compose them?"

"I learned it of my brother, sir, but it is the work of the bard Guesare."

"Guesare? He is one of my sister's friends, is he not?"

How does her brother know Guesare? wondered Blen. This was a new bit of information for him, another peep into the tangle of secrets around the two women he had been accompanying.

Fachalana recognized all this as well. She is teasing poor Blen, she thought. He so wants to know who she is.

"He is, my lord. He and my brother have ridden together at times in Lama."

The Lady Fachalana could scarce keep herself from giggling. "I did not know of this place, Modi," she said. "It looks as if everyone else forgot it too."

"It is in great disrepair. I fear many of these books are ruined from the damp." Modareth swung an arm toward the volumes lining the walls.

Donzalo would love this place, Blen thought.

"Are you up to a late supper, gentlefolk?" asked Carrana. "I have had what clothes you brought cleaned and laid out in your rooms. Refresh yourselves and please join the prince and me in an hour, won't you?"

~ ~ ~

To Donzalo's disappointment, Orgelo and his men bypassed Todmouth, cutting westerly across the countryside toward their home. The young knight had wanted to see Ros-town's greatest rival on the central Weldar.

"It is not much, really," Guesare told him, "not half the size of your town."

So Donzalo had heard before. Though the Tod was a major tributary to the Weldar, and a far mightier flow than the Abam, there was simply not that much trade coming down its stream. Ros-town stood central to all of Lama, amid its richest farmlands.

It also interested him that Todmouth was a free city, ruled by a lord mayor. None of the surrounding counties had been able to agree as to which should control the place so they had chosen this solution. The mayor, however, was appointed by the counts — who took turns naming him — and not elected by the folk of Todmouth.

The party, in time, reached the northern banks of the Tod.

Orgelo pointed out landmarks to his young guest, who rode beside him again on the last leg of their journey. This was a political consideration — the count wanted Donzalo at his side when he entered his own keep, as a symbol of his goodwill toward the Rosam.

"It is but a short way now to my home," said he, "where there is, naturally, a ford across the Tod. It is the first place one may safely cross the river." A sensible spot to place a keep, thought Donzalo.

"Have you given thought to putting a bridge across, my lord?" he asked.

"Why, when one can wade?" said the count. The concept seemed without merit to him. He had heard that Donzalo liked to build things and put it down to that.

"Up that way," the count went on, pointing north-westerly, "lie the lands of your cousin Daboreth. 'Tis poor country, at least as farm land, though I visit sometimes for the hunting.

"I have sent him word of your coming. I've no doubt he will visit."

The land through which they passed was quite rolling and there were many gullies washed into the hillsides. Cattle grazed here and there. Donzalo thought of treatises upon scientific farming he had read.

He knew by now that Orgelo would turn a deaf ear to such ideas.

Unlike Castle Rosam perched on its cliffs, Keep Arvaram spread upon a low hill near the river. It looked larger than his home at first, but Donzalo realized it did not rise so high and that it somewhat merged into the village around it. He could not help thinking how quickly a few cannon might level such a place.

Perhaps Sir Copago could tighten things up around here. He would have the ear of Orgelo's heir.

The muddy flow of the Tod reached not even to their stirrups. "Is the water higher at other times of the year, my lord?" he asked.

"Yes, boy, but very rarely impassible." The count laughed. "We really do not need your bridge."

~ ~ ~

Radal flown from the keep. On the wings of a dragon, no less, if one believed the reports.

King Lareth was glad the Lady Fachalana had already been on the road when it happened. He did not need her further complicated in this matter. Let the girl go enjoy some time in the countryside.

For a moment, he wondered what all this might mean for her supposed union with Jobareth Nafal. Lareth did not believe for a moment that either really wanted to marry the other and now they had no reason.

But that was not of great concern right now. What plans did Radal have, wherever he might have gone? They would center on the Rosam boy, of course, but would have wider implications. He must inform Lord Doufan as well as was possible and put trust in that man's abilities.

Lareth remembered his last interview with the ambassador before he left Celatas and the words Doufan had spoken to him then. Radal serves the king, he had said, but I serve the kingdom. The king smiled briefly at the memory – it was so like the man.

Let him now serve well.

He looked out from the battlements toward Lama. How often before had he done so? He would need men on the ground there. Radal had a company at his service, the king knew, and that threat must be countered. He would send trusted soldiers, a few at a time, to muster in the lands of Count Dordos.

Perhaps it would not be amiss to send a few through Doram Pass as well, and Sir Blen with them. Yes, he must send word and soldiers to the knight.

And have more men mustered here at Mountain Keep. He might yet, as he had once told his lord councilor, ride into Lama himself at the head of an army. It might be the only way to put things right.

## 3

"I myself drove the dagger into the old man," boasted Sojel. It was unusual for the sergeant to brag but it was unusual as well for him to be so drunk.

"We're going to see some real action now, my boys," said he. "The master has come and is ready to unleash us." Sojel knew not that his master no longer wielded any power in Sharsh and perhaps he would not have cared. His loyalty was all to Radal the man.

"You should have hanged many times over, Sergeant," said one of his ruffians.

"That goes for all of us," muttered another.

"But we haven't yet, have we?" asked Sojel, his high cheekbones — evidence of his Muram heritage — catching the glare of the fire. "We are kings until the moment we mount that scaffold, answering to none but ourselves and Asak."

There came grunts of agreement from around the blaze.

"Will he come here?" asked one.

"I know not and it is not mine to ask. I sent a couple fellows and a horse to him." The mercenary snickered. "Vanob's old mount. It's a good piece of horseflesh."

He rose, only a tad unsteadily. "We ourselves must move our camp in the morning. Be ready." Sergeant Sojel staggered off to find his bed and dreamless sleep.

~ ~ ~

Fachalana found herself staring at her hostess. There was something about her, something she sensed.

"Carrana" she asked, a bit uncertainly, "are you with child?"

Ansa glanced quickly and sharply toward her friend, and then back to the princess.

The woman nodded an assent. "How did you know, Lana? Has Modi been telling our secrets?"

"No, I just — knew it somehow."

Carrana looked pleased and a little frightened. Ansa could not fault her for the second; Fachalana scared her now and again, as well.

"Please let it go not further than we three. Modi does not want his father to know until we are safely back in the capital. He fears it would distract the king."

Ansa spoke up. "The prince has a head on his shoulders."

"When he chooses to use it," replied Carrana dryly. Fachalana laughed openly at the remark. That was very much the Modareth she had know all her life, bookish and full of knowledge, and often spectacularly impractical.

The Anian, not knowing him so well, did not laugh with her. "When are those boys getting back?" she asked.

"If they only tour the vineyard, in time for lunch," answered Carrana. "If they stop to sample its products, maybe never!"

~ ~ ~

Donzalo had only one room in the keep of Count Orgelo, but it was quite a large one. That seemed to be the norm here, in this rambling edifice.

"If we run out of space, we double and triple up," said the servant who had shown him to his quarters. "This way, we needn't build so many rooms."

Accordingly, the young knight told his bodyguard to move into the room with him. No one objected. They were rather a relaxed people here at Tod-ford.

Or a lazy people, said Habidros. The Cuddonian did not approve at all of their lax ways. "I could take this place with ten good men," he claimed, "and lose not a one of them."

To which Copago had replied, "They do not put much faith in fortifications. The soldiers of Count Orgelo are ready to ride quickly anywhere rather than hide behind walls."

Donzalo did not envy Sir Copago his task here. That knight was, indeed, immediately made master of arms for Sorsen's household. In that Sir Sorsen rarely remained home, this meant Copago would do much traveling.

All knew that Sir Copago was very much a homebody. He might

not soon send for his family when he must live in so unsettled a manner.

"Sir Donzalo," called Sorsen, as he came down to the great central hall on his second morning. It was higher than the hall at Castle Rosam, a full two stories with an arcade around the upper level, and built all of rough-hewn logs. "Come greet your cousin Daboreth."

"Hail, Cousin," said the man. Donzalo remembered the young count from a visit he had made to County Rosam. It had been for Ros's naming, near a year and a half ago, hadn't it?

"My greetings to you, Count Daboreth," said he. Despite his title, this cousin of his held sway over less land than Donzalo's own uncle.

Sir Sorsen stepped between them and wrapped an arm around each man's shoulders. Sorsen was of more than normal height, but still had to reach up a bit for Donzalo. "Come have some breakfast.

"Ho, you," he called to a passing servant. "Have food sent for we three. Eggs. Plenty of eggs. Come on, kinsmen."

Donzalo had never greatly cared for Sorsen's bluff persona — which he suspected was at least partly assumed — and could see that his cousin had similar feelings. But one must put up with things from ones host.

Sorsen released the two when a guardsman came hurrying up to him. After a brief, low conversation, he said, "My apologies, I must let you breakfast alone. There is word of bandits crossing our lands." He grabbed a large piece of beef from the plate of a man seated nearby and rushed out the doors, gnawing upon it.

"By bandits, he means smugglers who have not paid the proper bribes," remarked the count. "Shall we eat?"

Shortly, a boy from the kitchen came to them with three plates. When he saw there were only two men, he shrugged and left the third portion sitting on the table.

There were, indeed, plenty of eggs, along with the beef that seemed to appear at every meal in Keep Arvaram. The bread that accompanied them was, in Donzalo's opinion, heavy and of rather low quality.

That did not prevent him from starting on the absent Sorsen's plate when he had finished his own. Donzalo found that he had an appetite this morning.

His cousin watched for a while, clearly amused but polite. As Donzalo remembered, Daboreth was a somewhat retiring sort, not inclined to initiate a conversation. He was a bit that way himself, he had to admit.

"Are you staying long, Cousin?" he asked.

"Only a day or two," came the reply. "And you?"

"Haven't decided." They ate in silence a while longer.

"You would be welcome to visit my home," spoke Daboreth.

Donzalo nodded only, as a rather tough piece of steak was in his mouth at that moment. "I would be honored, Cousin," he responded, when able.

"Call me Dabbi. Everyone does."

"Donni." He looked at his cousin. "How soon can we get out of this place?"

Daboreth laughed, somewhat circumspectly at first and then more loudly, shaking his head. "As soon as possible," said he.

~ ~ ~

"It seems like an exchange of prisoners," joked Tiana. "You come here, I go there."

Tiana had a somewhat skewed sense of humor in Janona's view, but she could see her point.

"Do you truly think your husband will stay at Keep Rosam?" she asked.

"He blustered a great deal about only trying it out and insisted on me remaining here for now, but I have no doubt he will settle into the job. 'Twill keep him out of mischief until he calls for me." Tiana turned her eyes back to the knitting in her lap.

For just whom is she making those little boots? wondered Janona.

The third woman there said nothing. Sima mourned still in her heart for her lost Borrago and found it hard to be merry.

"Like my Copago, he is a man who feels called to his duty," said

Janona quietly. She too was mourning a loss, even if only a temporary one.

"Does anyone know what Grippo is up to?" asked Sima of a sudden. "I've barely seen him."

Janona had an answer. "When not attempting to unpack and organize all of Donzalo's books, Grippo has been serving as secretary to Sir Paren."

The older woman nodded her head. "He could find worse employ."

"He will be ordained someday, Mother, I am sure of it. If not here, in some other county by some other hierophant."

"Not among those Arvaram heretics, I would hope!" objected Sima.

The other two looked at each other; both had heard Brother Grippo express sentiments that might be seen as favoring the Lorjam Pontifex.

"Certainly not, Dame Sima," said Tiana, "most certainly not."

~ ~ ~

Radal had been able to bring only one thing with him, other than the dagger at his belt, the clothes he wore, and the small grimoire he kept always on his person. That was the ebony cask which held his most powerful object of magic. All the way here, clinging to the back of the dragon, he had made certain not to let it slip from him.

There were many other things in his tower, back at Mountain Keep, that he might have wished to bring, but the sorcerer could do without them. He could raise magics enough, here in this dusty, crumbling keep.

And he would.

But for now, he was depending on his human agents. Sojel had sent him a satisfactory mount, should he need it, and a couple of men to do his bidding. Soon more messengers would be going back and forth between Lord Radal and the sergeant, as well as his various spies. Not all those messengers need be human.

Then, there was Fachalana.

# THE SIGN OF THE ARROW

He had tried to make contact with his daughter. She was blocking him and, moreover, disappearing into some place he seemed unable to follow. That took great power.

Radal sighed. So it must be. He would never see his Fachalana again in the flesh but he could still hope to speak to her once more. Just once more.

## 4

Fachalana would not permit her father to link with her. Not now, not as things were. When he pressed too strongly she would take refuge in her silver world. She did not want to speak with him. She feared to speak with him.

Had he remained in Mountain Keep, not gone forward with his madness, she might have been open to Lord Radal. But the news had, in time, reached here of his flight.

With it came Sir Blen's new orders. She would miss the knight, even if he were a bit stuffy. Ansa would miss him, too, she was sure.

She heard a creaking in the courtyard below, and voices. Who might that be? The soldiers on guard knew not to let anyone in.

Oh, it was Murbalana and Doo with their cart, and the other soldier who had accompanied them to Lama. Who was that fourth fellow? He did look familiar.

"My luggage!" she exclaimed. "Maresta! Our luggage has arrived!"

She rushed to the cart to find her travel chest, the one with all the drawers and the top that became a vanity. Fachalana greatly missed that chest and its contents.

Ansa followed more cooly, and greeted the tired travelers. "Pol, isn't it?" asked she, when the young man climbed down from his steed.

"Yes, ma'am. You — you remember me?"

"Why, Jobareth Nafal told me you were his chosen man. How could I forget that?"

Pol felt quite puffed up at that moment.

As well he should, having shepherded this group across the mountains on less than well-maintained and somewhat dangerous roads.

"Is Sir Blen here, my lady?" he asked. He thought he should be making a report to someone official.

"Off preparing for his own trip across the mountains," Ansa told him. "He might want to take you back with him."

"Not soon, I hope. I am very tired of going up and down, ma'am!"

# THE SIGN OF THE ARROW

~ ~ ~

Daboreth did not truly have a keep at all, only a manor-house surrounded by a wooden palisade. The pair of cousins, accompanied by Habidros and the single attendant the count had brought with him, left the home of Orgelo as early as manners permitted the day following their meeting. They had spent much of that day in conversation, as Count Orgelo seemed to have quite forgotten his guests.

Guesare chose to remain behind, saying only that a private matter must claim his attention. Donzalo surmised that private matter was the handsome young fellow who sat enthralled by the minstrel's playing the night before.

Let Guesare have his flings. There was no need to burden Dabbi with another guest, anyway.

"Much of my day here is spent with my herds," said the count, as he gave them a tour of his holdings. How old is he? wondered Donzalo. Thirty, maybe, and he knew he had been count nearly a decade. His father must have passed when he was young. But then, so had Donzalo's, hadn't he?

"Have you a wife to help you with all this, Cousin?" he asked.

"Not yet. Count Orgelo keeps throwing his eligible relatives at me when I visit but I have been able to dodge them so far."

"I could find you someone suitable back home in no time," said Habidros. "A man like you is appreciated in the Cuddon." He sniffed at the air. "What is that stench?" Donzalo could smell it too.

"Oh, there is much brimstone on my lands. Where it rises to the surface, it ruins the grazing."

Donzalo and his bodyguard exchanged a meaningful look. "Might we see some of it?" asked the young knight.

The count shrugged. "If you wish. It's not useful for much other than curing the mange."

Soon they were surveying a hillside streaked with the near-pure mineral. "A treasure!" exclaimed Habidros. Daboreth was completely baffled.

"Know you not, man, that brimstone is an essential ingredient of gunpowder?" asked Donzalo.

"The other necessary components are easier to come by," added Habidros. "Yon woodlands would provide charcoal and your cattle could be a ready source of saltpeter."

Donzalo continued. "Much of the brimstone we use now must need come from Lorj. I hear there are great mines in the north-west of the island."

"They are closest thing on earth to Asak's realm, says Guesare. He has viewed them," said Habidros, "or claims to have."

"Even with his customary exaggerations, I would not doubt it," replied Donzalo, who had read of those mines. He turned to his kinsman. "You are wealthier than you know, Dabbi. Far wealthier."

The nobleman stared at his young cousin. "What am I to do?"

"We can think of some things," replied Donzalo, with a wink to the Cuddonian. "Let us get back to your manor so we might discuss them."

~ ~ ~

Ros had again climbed to the top of the divan, standing perched there. He growled.

"He must be a tiger today, my lady," said Traspa. "I dare not get close to the boy for he will surely pounce on me."

"Ros! Get down from there." He only growled more loudly at his mother.

"He can be obstinate," observed the maid. "It is good that he is speaking some now but I wish that he knew other words than *no*."

"That is perhaps the best word a ruler can know," observed Count Bolos from the doorway.

"Husband, I did not know you were there." Lomela put aside her embroidery and went to kiss him on the cheek. She could smell the wine on his breath. "You do not visit here much anymore."

"I know, I know." Bolos shrugged. "And I've no good excuse." He held out his arms to his heir, who leaped into them with a great roar. The count dropped onto the couch with the boy in his lap.

"Our Corgos has decided to stay," be said, "and has sent for his wife. She will come down with my uncle when next he visits. What boy, you are a pick-pocket now?" He removed Ros's hands from the purse hanging at his belt. "Ha, he was able to untie the strings!"

"He is clever, my lord," offered Mistress Traspa.

"I know nothing of this Tiana he has married but I think the happiness of my master of arms depends upon the happiness of his wife. I would have her feel welcome here."

"She will live in the keep?" asked Lomela.

"Aye. No living outside the walls for Sir Corgos. The man likes to be close to his work." He put the boy down beside him. "I am going to put the both of them in my old rooms. Please do help her find her way about, won't you, my lady?"

"Most assuredly, my husband. It will be good to see new faces." Indeed, it would, she said to herself. This place has been dull lately.

Ros growled again and started to climb the back of the divan.

~ ~ ~

It was not proving to be as profitable a season as Galaro and his company had hoped. Many called for pulling out of the fair as soon as possible.

"Let's stick it out another week, boys," said the Cuddonian. "If things are no better, I'll be first to start packing up."

It was Bolos and his suspicions that was hurting everything. Yes, the death of old Borrago and the cancellation of the tourney had put a damper on the fair, but trade had been good enough until someone shot at the new count.

Now he was banishing traders for no reason and arresting honest travelers to be questioned up in the keep. That was no way to do business. Count Borrago had known that, despite his exorbitant fees and tariffs. They might grumble but the merchants could live with those, aye, and make a profit too.

If too many did decide to pull out of the Summer Fair, the whole thing might collapse. This was the hub for trade throughout central

Lama, and much of what lay beyond. It was where merchants from all over bought their wholesale goods to carry far and wide.

"One more week," he told them again, "and we'll see."

## 5

"I had mused upon gunpowder production while at my uncle's keep," Donzalo told the man seated across the large round table from him. The table, like much of the furniture in Daboreth's home, was of pine brought down from the mountains. Indeed, as was much of Daboreth's home itself. "He certainly has enough trees to provide the charcoal and I have heard of brimstone deposits across the hills of the Cuddon in the lower Siph valley."

"Which is thoroughly in Anian hands," objected Habidros, seated to his left. "I'm not sure how they would feel about that plan."

"The Ani, as everyone else, like to make a profit, Habi. If it were worth their while, they would send their brimstone over the hills.

"But this is better."

"What of the saltpeter?" asked Daboreth.

"There are methods to extract it from the dung of your cattle," said Habidros. "You've plenty enough of that."

Donazalo spoke. "Back home, there are caves in the hills rising to the Cuddon. Those caves are full of bats and their droppings. That's the best source."

"Aye," agreed Habidros, "or at least the easiest to gather."

The fourth man at the table was the count's master of arms. Here, that title meant essentially foreman. The leathery fellow felt that firearms would never replace the bow and was cool to this entire discussion. The idea of profits, however, did keep him interested. His master, if not exactly impoverished, could use a better cash flow.

"So are we talking about making this gunpowder here or at County Rosam?" he asked.

"Here, I would think," said Donzalo. "My brother would not approve one of my projects right now."

He looked to his cousin. "It will take money to get started. And do not think of asking old Orgelo for it."

"No, Donni, when he was done there would be money nowhere but in his own pockets."

To the surprise of all, the man of arms made a most astute comment. "Sharsh might be interested. We are near the southern pass here and I'm sure they would like a source other than the Coradeans."

Habidros nodded in agreement. "They would buy just the brimstone. You wouldn't need make the powder here at all."

Donzalo did not like that idea, even while recognizing its merits. He so wanted to make gunpowder!

"More profit in making it in Lama and selling it in Lama," he argued. "Why give it to Lareth for a few pennies?" Especially when it could be used in those cannons he had long imagined back in County Rosam.

Habidros took a gulp from his tankard. He didn't know how these Lamans could stand to drink this thin, warm ale. "This talk of the pass interests me. Is it much used?"

"Orgelo tries to discourage its use in various ways," asserted Count Daboreth. "It is to his advantage to have trade come around the mountains in the south so he can better control it. Still," he continued, "there is always some traffic."

"More in the winter, when the northern route is less attractive," added the master of arms.

"The way to it runs through the lands of my neighbor to the north and he is no friend of Orgelo," said Daboreth. "Not that he likes me much, either."

"It's just your misfortune to be stuck between them, boss," observed the count's master of arms.

"Well," said Donzalo, "we are not going to build a gunpowder factory tonight, nor even on the morrow. This will take much planning.

"But, Dabbi, it might not be a bad idea to start gathering brimstone that can be refined when the time comes."

"And maybe some cow patties as well," suggested Habidros. "The stench of one can cover the stink of the other!"

~ ~ ~

Pol sipped from his goblet. "It's passable, I suppose."

"Spoken like a true son of Arolin," laughed Sir Blen. "This wine of Dor is an acquired taste, I think."

"It's unrefined," Pol asserted. "Too sweet, too strong — too *everything*."

"We need the expert opinion of the legate. He made you a sergeant, eh?"

"I think it was somewhat in jest, sir."

"Even his jests have meaning. He is far more calculating than one might realize." And he recognized potential in this lad. "I grew up in the valley of the lower Chas and what wine we produce there is only sold in the local taverns.

"Have you family in Arolin?"

"All dead, sir, slain by marauding Muram soldiers."

"Ah." The two sat in silence for a while, in the shade of a great magnolia that grew just without the keep's low walls. I would have this cut down, thought Blen. There should be no cover for enemies to approach.

"I have a dilemma, Pol," said the knight. "I must cross into Lama with the men we are being sent, yet I do not like leaving the ladies here without a guardian. Not to mention the prince, himself."

"Might I trust you to remain here in my stead?"

"What would I know of such a commission, sir? Are there not soldiers stationed here?"

"That is what they are — soldiers. You have shown you can be more, lad." A slight smile came to Blen's face. "A fairly able spy, for one thing. It took me a while, but I have seen through your subterfuges, Pol. You had me underestimating you.

"So, be my spy here and keep an eye on those two."

The boy actually wanted to stay, didn't he? I think he will do well, and it is not that great a matter, after all.

"Now you must tell me of your journey here. Everything, so I may know what to expect across the mountains."

~ ~ ~

"Welcome back, my boy. How were things at Daboreth's?"

156

"Interesting, my lord — for a while." He had been gone, between travel and visit, a full week.

"Life can grow boring at his place. He's a good man. Needs a wife, though. I'll find him one he likes one of these days!" Count Orgelo gave his guest an appraising look. "Perhaps you could use a bride, too. Have you met my sister's daughter?"

Donzalo had seen the woman in question and thought she looked altogether too much like Sir Sorsen. "I am but a younger son, on the road and with little prospects at the moment," he said. "Perhaps someday."

The answer satisfied the count. "So, will you remain with us a while, Sir Donzalo?"

"I am not certain, my lord. Perhaps I should see what my friend Guesare wishes to do."

"Oh, the minstrel grew bored too and set off for Todmouth yesterday. Says he may await his brother there, or go meet him on the road."

"Hmm, I have wanted to see that town. Perhaps, sir, I shall ride down myself in a day or two."

"'Tis a mean place, Donzalo, full of filth and whores. I am sure you would much prefer the company of my niece."

~ ~ ~

They knew the boy had gone south with Count Orgelo. Beyond that, there was little intelligence.

He must send out scouting parties. Sojel wanted to be out himself, rather than sitting here awaiting orders. His second could do that.

The sergeant craved action. He would take a couple men and head toward Todmouth. He could set up a sort of headquarters there, where his spies in the region might report to him.

And Sojel might, perhaps, find things to divert himself in that town.

Best he make a wide swing around that little village, though, and cross somewhere else. Someone just might recognize him from his last visit there. It would have been dangerous to have a large body of men on the road after that — patrols always increased after such incidents.

But they also always forgot them, didn't they, sooner or later?

~ ~ ~

Summer Fair had limped along for another week, even regaining some of its vigor, but Galaro knew it was time to take to the road.

"We stuck it out for three weeks, men, and made our profits," he said to his assembled company. "Not the profits we might have liked but not so bad, either.

"So I put it to you: do we go or remain for the last week of the fair?"

"Let's pack it up," said one.

"Agreed."

"Aye, the road calls!"

Not one voice spoke to the contrary.

"Then we go, lads," announced the burly trader. "And good riddance to Ros-town until next year. May we find more profits then!"

"To profits!" came an answering voice, accompanied by cheers and the raising of many flagons. The men quickly dispersed and began the methodical and efficient loading of their wagons.

## 6

It was good to have money in his pockets but Perdos remained frugal. Maybe he could use it to rebuild the burned-out inn when he finished his business. That would be a fitting use for the innkeeper's cash.

Yes, he could see himself there, greeting customers from behind the bar. Why not Hendel in the kitchen? The cook would probably be interested in investing in a real inn rather than manning a stall by the river. And a wife by his side and maybe kids who would grow to help out around the place.

Stop daydreaming, he told himself, and pay attention to the work at hand. Sir Perdos doubted it would do much good to travel up the Tod in hope of learning anything. He did not know the country well enough and it was, moreover, mostly open countryside that offered little concealment for him. Best he stay here in town for a few days, take a room at *The Truculent Troll*, and listen to what gossip there might be.

He let his hand rest on the hilt of his long sword. Would he ever get to use it on Guesare?

And once he got that chore out of the way, he would very much like to bury it in the gut of Sojel.

~ ~ ~

The crossing was not difficult on horseback but Blen saw that it might not have been quite so simple for Pol and the cart he had escorted. The way was often narrow, often steep. Rock falls seemed commonplace and one must either try to get around them or attempt to move them.

It seemed that neither Sharsh nor Count Mussago on the Laman end was particularly interested in maintaining the road. He remembered Nafal talking about it, that the legate's family would like to see more trade pass through here. Blen was not sure he would want to transport wagon-loads of wine across Doram Pass.

Mussago knew to expect him and his troop of two twenties, and would give them safe passage. That money had exchanged hands, Sir

Blen had no doubt. They could encamp near his southern border and wait.

Blen's duty here was to keep an eye on Count Orgelo's movements, should trouble arise in Lama. Their host apparently was not fond of County Arvaram and its lord and just might add some of his own troops to those of Sharsh, if he felt the need.

They now descended into Lama. It was poor scrubby country here. Could there once have been forest covering these hills, long since cut and not replaced?

He looked to his map. There was a town at the confluence of the Tod and Weldar. It would not do to take a large body of men into such a place but he might send one or two to listen for any news.

He might even go himself.

~ ~ ~

This latest bit of news his spies had brought him intrigued Radal. It seemed that his daughter had ridden out to meet the king, without telling him, and imparted some great secret to Lareth.

King Lareth had told him he had new intelligence about Donzalo, a secret that changed everything, when he came to him later that day, hadn't he? Had that information come from Fachalana? If only he could speak to the girl!

The prophecy — it had spoken of Donzalo's son. Was there something there he should know? Did the boy have a bastard somewhere of whom they had been unaware?

No point in wondering. But this might be the reason Fachalana refused his link so steadfastly. She could be afraid of revealing too much.

There were ways he could force her but he did not wish to use them on his daughter. She was not strong enough to withstand him if he brought all his powers to bear but what might become of her own mind if he did so? No, he dare not take that path.

But he would destroy Donzalo. That had not changed.

~ ~ ~

"I intend to have all these songs in a book," said Prince Modareth. "I know a good printing house in Celatas."

"The one Jobareth uses?" asked Lady Fachalana.

The prince had been taking down every lay and ballad Ansa knew. The Anian knew quite a few, and that did not include the ones in her native language.

"Yes, that is the one, my lady."

Pol was never quite certain of his place here. He knew he was not part of this noble circle and did not try to be. But Blen had asked him to take his place and that meant keeping close to them. The foursome would have included him without thinking but allowed him his reticence.

So he usually stayed in corners or near doors, eyes open for anything he thought seemed dangerous. He was exceedingly meticulous in this.

"It is too bad we can not show the tunes somehow," spoke Carrana.

"Most, my lady," said Ansa, "are old and traditional melodies. Minstrels have been reusing them for centuries."

"Still, my wife is right," Modareth said. "There are ways of writing down the tunes but none of us here know them. My brother's wife," he continued, "can sit down with a piece of paper before her and play a tune from it, even one she has never heard before!"

"Our son must be taught to do that," said Carrana, taking her husband's hand.

"Or daughter, my dear," he replied. "You appear tired."

"Yes, Modi, I think I'd best to bed."

"I too, then. I bid you good night, my ladies."

As the royal couple departed the room, Ansa leaned close to Fachalana and whispered, "I think our Pol is rather cute, don't you?"

"I thought you liked Blen, " was the reply.

"May I not think they are both handsome men?" objected Ansa. "And Blen is far away now."

Such an attitude seemed frivolous to Fachalana.

Pol seemed to be alert to something, cocking an ear upward. "Are there more squirrels in the ceiling?" asked Ansa.

"I — do not think so, my lady." The young man turned and ran toward the stair.

~ ~ ~

Guesare rode beside the wide, muddy River Tod. Its course had run almost due south for some distance, before making a great loop back to the east to join the Weldar.

The Cuddonian could have followed a road that cut across that loop and would have carried him back to the river at its mouth, but he was in no hurry. Guesare wished to see the Tod in all its length, though it would add the better part of a day to his travel. Down here the soil was richer and farm fields lay on either side of the water.

Was this still part of Count Orgelo's land? He wasn't quite sure where it ended but knew it did not include Todmouth. The minstrel didn't remember any border guards along the way but they were lax about that sort of thing in the south. County Arvaram's borders were too long and Orgelo's soldiers too few to ever hope to seal them.

There were shanties along the road now, slums on the outskirts of Todmouth. A slatternly woman stood before one and beckoned to him. Guesare shook his head politely. *Not my type*, he laughed to himself.

As he remembered, there were three taverns in the town. Yes, and the one across the river. There was the *Troll*, of course. That was the best. Oba's place, down near the docks, was thoroughly disreputable and no place for him.

*The Count's Cow* lay a little further from the center of town, which meant it was both cheaper and quieter. The clientele, when he had visited before, tended to be working men from the country, drovers, teamsters. That should be his destination.

Such men were likely to have news for him. They were just the sort to buy him a drink for singing a sentimental song, too.

162

## 7

There was a shadow with a sword.

Pol was no great swordsman but he rushed the man, swinging his own blade. It caught the surprised would-be assassin on his left arm as he turned to flee. The young Arolinian threw himself at the man's legs and brought him to the floor.

By that time, Fachalana had caught up to him, a dainty dagger in her own hand, and, not far behind her, Ansa with a pair of guardsmen.

Once the two soldiers had taken charge of his captive, Pol said, "I heard a noise, his scabbard on the windowsill, I think, and then the sound of steel being drawn from the scabbard. That sound I would know anywhere."

The prince stood silhouetted in his doorway, the Princess Carrana behind him. He looked at Pol a moment and then held out his hand.

"Give me your sword, man," said he, "and kneel."

He tapped the young soldier on each shoulder, saying, "I name you Sir Pol, Knight of Sharsh," and handed back the weapon.

"From this time you must be ever at my side, Sir Pol." The prince smiled toward the girls. "I can not expect the Lady Fachalana to be my full-time bodyguard, after all."

"Pol has gifts, too," whispered Ansa to her friend, "and I still think he is cute."

"He must have come over the wall," said the captain when he came to make his report. He appeared quite perturbed that he had let an assassin nearly reach his royal charge. "Sir Blen was right. I need to take down all those trees."

"And double your guard, " said Fachalana. The man nodded in agreement.

Modareth glared at the soldier from beneath raven brows. The lady could see that the prince was seething, barely containing his anger. He had always had a temper and could be prone to outbursts. It is good that he is managing to control it, she thought.

How like his eyes are to his father's, she also thought, to no particular purpose.

"You must learn who the man is," demanded the prince. "Have you questioned him yet?"

"He says nothing — so far. He seems to be Muram."

Pol spat at the mention of that name but did not speak.

"I would guess him a hired sword," continued the captain. "He is unlikely to know anything beyond who handed him his blood money."

"That would be a start," Modareth said. "Let us hope it is not also an end."

~ ~ ~

Princess Mara looked her husband up and down.

"It is a good choice, my husband. No, an excellent choice."

"Once I wear them in public, there is no going back, you know. Our colors will be forever green and gold."

"They both honor your father and mark you your own man, Gawis. I think they are perfect." Mara did not add that she liked the way they went with his straw-colored hair.

"I hope he sees it that way."

"I hope he sees all the changes in you," she said. "You will be a great king, Husband."

"A king is only as great as those who stand with him. This I have learned lately and I think it may be the most important thing I might know."

He took his wife into his arms and kissed her brow. "Let us pray to Jov that it will be a time yet before I wear the crown."

Princess Mara did not pray to Jov, being a good Kamatian, but she shared her husband's sentiment.

~ ~ ~

How this mud sucked at his feet! Were the streets ever dry in Todmouth?

Guesare had dismounted and now led his pony up a backstreet. It would not do to let the steed hurt himself in this mire. He remembered this way as a shortcut to the inn, his destination.

"So, Sir Guesare. Well met!" Before him stood Lord Radal's right hand man, Sojel. He sensed more than saw the two ruffians who had moved into the street behind him.

The minstrel stepped away from his mount to give himself room to move. There was not time to reach the saddle and attempt to bolt out of this trap. They would have him down in the mud if he tried.

"Your overlarge charge is not with you? Still up at Orgelo's place I would guess." The sergeant sneered. "We can deal with him later.

"But you have been a hindrance to my master all along. He will thank me for removing you." Sojel, holding the heavy, curved blade he favored, began to circle to his left. Guesare knew the men behind him were moving too.

One rushed in and he turned to parry his attack, to be nearly overwhelmed by the other. And Sojel was circling, ready to strike when he saw an opening. That opening would inevitably come; Guesare could not fight three swordsmen. Especially not when this muck impeded his movement.

'Tis too bad none is here to commemorate my last battle, he told himself. I will attempt to make it a memorable one.

Or was there someone there?

Sojel had turned to face a newcomer. Guesare almost did not recognize the man for a moment, without his beard. Did he now face four opponents?

Then let this last battle be his best.

~ ~ ~

It seemed that life at Castle Rosam was starting to return to normal. Perhaps the presence of the new master of arms had something to do with it. The competent Corgos was straightening out much of the chaos of the past month.

Bolos, too, was beginning to settle down and again allowing visitors to the keep. Jobareth had not been there in weeks, not since the funeral.

It looked the same as he rode through the inner gate but it was not. A new count sat in Borrago's chair. Many of his old friends were gone, and some might never return.

But Lomela remained, his princess. Ultimately, did he really care about anything else here? His job as a diplomat was only a job, even if he rose to the top of the government some day. He lived still to serve her, as he had as a boy.

What a fool you are, Jobareth Nafal, he told himself. He wondered then if he should still marry the Lady Fachalana. Would there be any reason now?

But then again, why not?

A groom took his reins. He should present himself first to the count, even if this were not an official call. The old informality would not do, maybe never again.

Just where did Bolos have his offices now, anyway?

## 8

"Perdos?" Surprise and rancor mingled in Sojel's voice.

The tall knight had drawn his long, heavy sword, and faced mercenary and minstrel. But which man would he attack?

He saw the faces of the little innkeeper and his wife before him, and knew that Percos must wait for his vengeance. He would have understood. "Forgive me, Brother," murmured Sir Perdos and launched a fierce attack upon Sojel.

Guesare had no time for astonishment, as the other two were again upon him. Perhaps this pair he could deal with; they were not mean swordsmen but neither were they his equals.

Sojel was a skilled duelist, and a ferocious one, but he could not get inside the sweep of the long sword where he might do damage. He saw from the corner of his eye that one of his men was down, as he again caught the force of that blade on his own.

"Murderer!" hissed Perdos. He recognized that he hated the Mur more than any other man in the world, Guesare included. As much as his father. A great overhand swing batted the sword from Sojel's numbed hand. "Monster!" Another roundhouse half-severed the man's body. He lobbed the head from it before the torso hit the ground.

He looked about the street. The other two assailants lay dead and Guesare stood facing the knight, holding his sword defiantly before him, and bleeding from a great gash on his left shoulder.

Perdos looked at the wounded man. This was not how he wanted his revenge.

"Sir Guesare," he said, "we will not cross swords today. But the next time I see you I shall surely kill you."

~ ~ ~

Habidros shook his head. "We can not let you out of our sight, Brother!"

"You might well have been arrested if Sojel — or what was left of him — had not been recognized as an outlaw," added Donzalo. "And Count Orgelo's man here put in a good word for you."

"Is it true that this Perdos I've heard about rescued you?" asked Habidros.

"Without him I would have been lying dead in the mud, I have no doubts. But I do not understand it." The minstrel, an arm once again in sling, looked about the tavern's common room. "Where do we go from here?

"Orgelo could provide us passports if you would care to travel south. Or would you prefer to head back to your home, Donni?"

"Maybe both, in time, but for now, let's go enjoy the hospitality of Count Orgelo a bit longer and wait for Galaro to arrive."

"His niece will approve of that," observed Habidros.

# AFTERWORD

I hope you have enjoyed this, the third book in the saga of Donzalo's Destiny. The story will be continued in upcoming books.

This fantasy novel is set in a world and time of its own, although it most closely resembles 16th Century Central Europe. The stories and characters, the world in which they "exist," arise from ideas I have played with for many years.

Incidentally, if one wishes to pronounce the names in this book, it is generally safe to treat them as one would Spanish — at least the names that come from the widely-spoken Muram language.

*Stephen Brooke*


Author and artist Stephen Brooke lives and works in an old farm-house in the Florida Panhandle. *The Sign of the Arrow* is his tenth book.

All are available from Arachis Press, a small publisher dedicated to presenting meaningful literature for readers of all ages. Visit http://arachispress.com for our catalog.


The *Donzalo's Destiny* epic fantasy
by Stephen Brooke consists of four books:
I. The Song of the Sword
II. The Shadow of Ask
III. The Sign of the Arrow
IV. The Hand of the Sorcerer